The Nightingale Detective Agency

Denise Devine

USA Today Bestselling Author

A 1920s Cozy Mystery

Book One

A Charlotte Van Elsberg Mystery

Wild Prairie Rose Books

The Nightingale Detective Agency

A 1920s cozy mystery with secrets worth killing for…

St. Paul, 1926—where ambition comes at a cost, especially for a woman.

Charlotte Van Elsberg is determined to become the city's first female private investigator and help women in need. She's already landed her first case: a grieving mother who wants answers about her daughter, Eleanor Kimball, a debutante killed in a suspicious car crash. Was it truly an accident or something more sinister? Char intends to find out. There's just one hitch—Char's husband.

Will Van Elsberg, a seasoned investigator, knows the job too well. It's no profession for a petite young lady, and he's not about to let his wife charge headfirst into danger. Char has other ideas. She agrees to hire bodyguards to satisfy his objections.

However, despite the addition of her "new team," she soon learns that this job is a lot harder than it appears. Doors slam in her face, alibis don't add up, and everyone appears to be hiding *something*. Does she have the grit and determination it takes to solve this case?

The more she digs into Eleanor's carefully polished life, the more she uncovers the young woman's secrets. Hidden truths that someone is desperate to keep buried. Evidence worth killing for. Now that Char is asking questions, who is determined to stop her from revealing the missing pieces?

Let's keep in touch!

Sign up for *Denise's Diary*, my monthly newsletter at:
https://www.deniseannettedevine.com/newsletter
Be the first to know about my new releases, sales and special events.

Chapter One

October 25, 1926

St. Paul, Minnesota

Carling's Uptown Café was the cat's meow—an elegant Louis XV-style dining room with towering French windows, velvet drapes, and glittering crystal chandeliers. When Ethel Rogers invited me to luncheon there, I could hardly refuse. Carling's was one of the most exclusive restaurants in St. Paul, and I had always wanted to sample their celebrated menu.

"I have a noon reservation under the name of Rogers," I said politely as I approached the maître d'hotel at twelve o'clock sharp. I'd taken great care to dress appropriately for such an elegant place, selecting a black silk chiffon drop-waist dress, black strap pumps, and a matching cloche hat. Pearls adorned my neck and ears. I had already removed my velvet cape coat and given it to the coat check girl.

The tall, stately, gray-haired man projected elegance and refinement in his black, cutaway coat with striped trousers, a starched white shirt, and a black tie as he checked his ledger. "Are you Mrs. William Van Elsberg?"

"Yes, I am," I replied, masking my irritation at being identified by my marital status. For crying out loud, this was 1926! I was a modern woman, proud of my right to vote, to drive an automobile, and dress as I pleased. I loved my husband dearly, but I was no one's property.

"Mrs. Rogers has already checked in. Right this way, please."

He led me to an elegantly set table with white linen, china accoutrements, and crystal goblets. Ethel Rogers sat across from me, munching on a plate of assorted canapés as he seated me and spread my napkin across my lap.

Ethel and I hadn't seen each other in a while and had a lot to catch up on, but the moment she greeted me, I sensed this wasn't going to be two dames clucking over the latest high-society scandal. Ethel's taut smile appeared forced, suggesting her usual air of confidence was a little off today. She definitely had something other than gossip on her mind.

"Char," Ethel said with a generous smile. "It's good to see you. How have you been?"

A wealthy woman in her sixties who had inherited a chunk of her father's iron ore mining fortune, Ethel always dressed as though she had a standing date with Douglas Fairbanks, that swashbuckling actor on the silver screen who had women swooning across America. Today she wore a teal, custom-tailored wool crepe suit paired with a silky, white bow blouse. Stone-gray hair set in flawless finger waves framed her face while a diamond and aquamarine comb anchored the thick chignon at her nape. She was old enough to be my mother, but the difference in our ages didn't bother me. Ethel was one of the sharpest, most outspoken women I knew. And that was precisely why I liked her.

True to form, she wasted no time pointing out that for a joint this expensive, her chair wobbled, the starched white tablecloth sat askew, the silver could use more polishing, and the crystal showed water spots. Yet it was what she didn't say that unsettled me. Despite her brisk, appraising chatter, she seemed unusually distracted. I wished I knew what was bothering her.

"How are your plans coming along?" Ethel asked during the main course. "The last time we talked, you were excited about starting an all-female detective agency."

"With the new baby and all, I'm afraid I haven't made much headway," I admitted. "I've been spending a lot of time with Nora Rose, getting to know her."

After Will and I returned from our honeymoon in late September, we became foster parents to a fifteen-week-old, orphaned baby girl. I also had an eleven-month-old son, Julien, by my late husband, Gus, so my days were joyfully full of bottles, lullabies, and tiny footsteps. Will and I had already decided to adopt Nora and instructed my attorney to file the petition.

"Goodness, let the nanny do her job," Ethel stated boldly as she adjusted her gold, wire-rimmed glasses. "I've got important investigative work for you to do." Glancing around to make sure no one was listening, she leaned forward. "Three days ago, my good friend, Marjorie Kimball, lost *her* daughter in a horrendous car crash. She's beside herself with grief, and she needs answers."

My fork stopped mid-air. "Ethel, that's awful. I'm so sorry."

Ethel frowned, her deep brown eyes intensifying. "Well, my dear, that's where you come in. The police have ruled it an accident. You need to uncover the truth of what *really* happened."

I nearly choked on my delicious roast chicken with chestnut stuffing. Grabbing my goblet, I drank some chilled lemon water to clear the errant bite stuck in my throat. Swallowing hard, I quickly dabbed my lips with my napkin and stared at her in disbelief. "You want me to do…what?"

"I want *you* to investigate the death of Eleanor Kimball." Ethel's deep, commanding voice held an air of authority as she leveled a bejeweled finger at me.

So, this was what she really asked me to lunch to talk about.

"She was murdered," Ethel continued, the conviction in her voice piercing the small space between us. "Well…" She paused, the lines etched on her brow deepening. "In my opinion, anyway. Marjorie believes that, too."

"Why do you think she was murdered?" I asked quietly and shoved my plate aside to lean closer to her to keep our conversation private.

"The car veered off the road at top speed and crashed into a tree, killing Eleanor instantly. She was a skilled driver and would never lose control. That's why Marjorie believes the accident is suspicious," Ethel replied and scooped up her last forkful of mashed potatoes and gravy, relishing it with gusto. "They found Eleanor alone in the car behind the wheel, but she *wasn't* alone when it crashed." Ethel clenched her manicured fingers into a fist. "An eyewitness said he saw two people in that car arguing as it sped past him while he was walking his dog. Whoever caused that crash fled on foot after the accident."

My mouth gaped in surprise. "What about the police? Surely, they're pursuing the eyewitness to corroborate the person's story."

Ethel shook her head in disgust. "They did interview him. They concluded that because he was old and had bad eyesight, he wasn't a credible witness. The case was labeled an accident and closed. I've got faith in you, Char, to find out who caused that crash and why they left her to die. Eleanor deserves justice."

I set down my fork and knife as my mind spun, trying to understand why she considered me qualified to take on a possible murder case. "But why me? Though the idea is certainly intriguing, I don't know anything about investigating such things yet."

Ethel speared a crisp green bean with her fork. "You told me you wanted to become a private investigator, like Will. Marjorie needs answers. You need a case to get started. There you are." She stuffed the green bean in her mouth and nodded as she chewed, as if her reasoning made perfect sense. Maybe to her, but…

I sipped my water, wondering how I would explain this sudden development to my husband. "Will and I haven't talked much about my becoming an investigator yet. He's been busy lately with a couple of pressing cases."

"Time is of the essence, my dear," Ethel said gravely. "You need to have that conversation with him so you can get started." Raising her hand, she snapped her fingers for the waiter to remove our empty plates.

Ethel's version of the story raised more questions than it answered, but I kept them to myself. Showing interest in the case might be taken as consent, and I needed to discuss this with Will first. The problem was, once Ethel got her foot in the door, there was no prying it out again.

Her faith in my ability as a fledgling to take on such an arduous task both flattered and terrified me. Yes, I wanted to become an investigator, and I wanted to help Marjorie Kimball, but at present, I knew next to nothing about investigating anything, much less a possible crime. I had planned on working with Will on a few cases to get experience first before striking out on my own. Looking into a suspicious death was a daunting undertaking for my first case.

"I agree that Eleanor deserves justice." As I spoke, a waiter's assistant deftly whisked away my plate, rearranged my dessert utensils, and set a beautiful china cup and saucer in front of me. "If the facts bear out that someone else caused the crash and then abandoned her, that person should be held accountable. I just don't know if I'm the right person—given my inexperience—to uncover the truth for her."

Our waiter silently appeared at the table with a silver urn of coffee. He poured the steaming liquid into my cup and handed me a small dessert menu.

"Darling, you have Will to consult," Ethel argued as she picked up the cream pitcher and poured a generous dollop into her coffee. "And I'll help you all I can."

She handed her unopened dessert menu back to the waiter. "I'll have the peach melba."

"I will, too," I chimed in as I handed him my menu. I was so shocked by Ethel's proposition that I couldn't concentrate on anything else, much less dessert.

After he left, I took a slow sip of my coffee, savoring its rich, bold flavor laced with a hint of chicory. The soft murmur of conversation and the faint clink of silver on china framed my thoughts as I mulled over my predicament. "Ethel, don't you think we're putting the cart before the horse? I don't have any references or experience yet to offer Marjorie Kimball."

"As I said, my dear, you have a husband who does," she replied encouragingly and reached across the table, squeezing my hand. "Will is one of the most trusted and thorough investigators in the Twin Cities. Surely, he'll give you advice whenever you need it."

"But Ethel, I don't have an office or business cards," I reasoned, giving my argument one last push. "I'm not set up to take cases yet."

"Leave it to me." With a wave of her hand, Ethel brushed my issues aside. "Willard and I own several office buildings. I'll take care of whatever you need. In the meantime, I'll set up a meeting with Marjorie to introduce you."

Her determined smile told me I wasn't getting out of this. My stomach tightened. I had no office, no training, no experience, and yet, Ethel wanted me to meet a total stranger and assure the woman in her hour of grief that I could give her closure. What if I failed because I was too new at this? The thought made my palms sweat. I'd been in tight spots before, but never one where someone else's peace depended on me. I hadn't even met the client yet, and I already knew I'd jumped in over my head. I had a lot to learn, and whatever training I received would probably be accomplished the hard way—from my mistakes.

The biggest challenge, however, wouldn't be the investigation itself or facing the client. It would be convincing my husband to let me try.

Chapter Two

That evening…

What began as an innocent after-dinner conversation while sitting in front of a crackling fire in the library of our home suddenly flared into a heated debate. In the six weeks since Will and I had married, we'd never quarreled, and the realization that neither of us intended to back down from this argument left me unsettled, but I couldn't let it go—not when I'd already given Ethel my word, albeit reluctantly, that I would meet with Marjorie Kimball to discuss Eleanor's accident.

"But Will," I cried, leaping from my leather wingback chair, so distraught that I could barely hold back my tears, "you're not listening to me!"

"That's not true. I heard every word you said," he replied in a deep, steel-soft tone. He rose and gently placed his large hands on my shoulders as he towered over me. "I love you, Char, and I want to make you happy, but I can't let you take on something that puts you in constant danger. My answer is still *no*."

Every inch of my five-foot, two-inch frame stood rigid as I clenched my fists and stared into my husband's intense blue eyes. A stray lock of thick, black hair had fallen across his brow, giving him that serious, thoughtful look I'd come to know all too well. "You're judging the situation before you have all the facts! Ethel and her friend, Marjorie Kimball, are counting on me to look into the cause of the crash involving her daughter's car. It's a simple inquiry. I'm not going to be in danger.

You've told me many times that you're just a guy who helps people solve their problems. That's what I'm trying to do, too."

Will's kohl brows furrowed in frustration. "Isn't that what your friend, Sally Wentworth, is doing by operating a home for homeless and abused women? If you want to help women, why don't you volunteer to work with her?"

It was true. My good friend, Sally, and the ladies of her church were doing a bang-up job running *Anna's House*, a refuge for women. I'd donated the building and remained their largest financial supporter.

"I'm already doing everything I can to give Sally and her crew whatever they need," I said. "If I showed up to volunteer every day, I'd just be getting in her way."

Still unconvinced, Will shook his head. "Domestic cases are unpredictable. They can spiral out of control in an instant. The same is true with murder investigations. You have no idea what you're walking into or who you're up against. It's too dangerous, Char."

My French-heeled pumps tapped across the polished wood floor, my garnet silk shift softly rustling as I hurried to make sure the library door was shut all the way. The floor-to-ceiling bookcases lining the walls overflowed with volumes of every sort, creating a soundproof barrier, but I needed to take extra precautions. I didn't want the servants to overhear our conversation, even though the effort was probably pointless. Somehow, they always seemed to know what went on in our house anyway.

"Of course, I know what I'm up against," I countered as I whirled around. "You're conveniently overlooking the fact that I'm the widow of a notorious bootlegger! Before the Feds shut down our nightclub, I supervised the main operation of La Coquette, and one of my jobs was to receive special guests and impress them with our hospitality. Some were distributors who purchased liquor through our bootlegging operation, and others were city officials who accepted bribes to look the other way. Gus had no shortage of crooked friends in the business, and I handled them like a champion."

"I don't doubt that you did an excellent job entertaining Gus' important clients. You're very good with people, but that's hardly on par with investigating them," Will stated flatly. "People in that crowd don't take kindly to someone poking into their personal lives. No one does."

I didn't like the way he kept twisting my words. "That's not what I meant, and you know it," I shot back. "What I'm trying to say is that I'm not some naive girl fresh off the farm. I'm a twenty-six-year-old woman who has a lot more experience dealing with people than most women my age. I realize I've still got a lot to learn, but I've never been afraid of a challenge. I aim to uncover the truth of what really happened in that crash and give a grieving woman the closure she deserves."

He closed his eyes and rubbed the back of his neck as if the strain of trying to reason with his headstrong wife took a toll on him. "Believe me, Char, investigating a case is not as easy or as smooth as you think," he replied sternly. "You get thrown out of joints, threatened, and roughed up by mugs who don't play nice. Sometimes, you get shot at. I've been through it all. I won't let you walk into that kind of jam on your own."

"But, Will, I won't be alone. Errol drives me everywhere—"

Gripping my arms, his eyes blazed with a mix of fear and frustration. "Darling, listen to me! Errol is a chauffeur, not a trained guard. Every time you leave the house, I worry that one of Gus' enemies is waiting to grab you to get a slice of his fortune. And you—" his voice roughened, "you're so darn stubborn. You think you can handle anything, but every time you charge ahead on your own, I'm left wondering if the next time you leave, it'll be the last time I see you alive."

Will was a level-headed guy and rarely lost his temper, but I knew that if I kept arguing, he would dig in his heels and permanently refuse to budge. I had to make him see my point because this was one dispute I couldn't afford to lose. Mrs. Kimball needed answers. Ethel had promised to supply everything she could to help me get my detective agency started. I couldn't let them down.

As much as I loathed the idea, it was time to pull out my trump card. Anxious to take the temperature down a notch, I moved close and slid my arms around Will's broad, muscular shoulders, curling them around his neck and feeling the crisp cotton of his starched white collar beneath my fingers. I smiled lovingly as I gazed into his eyes. "Look, I realize that working as an investigator isn't a walk in the park. It's probably even more risky for a dame. That's why I…" I drew in a deep breath, willing myself to confess the words aloud. "I'll agree to having bodyguards escort me. Everywhere. All the time."

He pulled back and stared at me as though I'd lost my mind. "You've been fighting me on this subject for months. What changed? I know how much you hate the idea. Whenever I bring it up, you never let me forget how Gus wouldn't allow you to go anywhere without his paid gorillas breathing down your neck, deciding where you could go and with whom you could socialize."

I shrugged, trying to act unperturbed even though my pulse raced at the thought of having to subject myself to such constant scrutiny again. My late husband had been adamant about my safety, never allowing me to go anywhere without a cadre of bodyguards surrounding me. Gus was probably turning in his grave at my independence now.

Gus had left me a Summit Avenue mansion, a business empire, and more money than I could ever spend, but even though I didn't care how rich I was, obviously, other people, especially Gus' sworn enemies, thought my wealth made me an attractive target. That was why Will insisted I still needed protection.

"Around-the-clock bodyguards were Gus' way of keeping me safe," I said truthfully, "but I hated being treated like a prisoner. I had no one to turn to. No one I could trust. I want to be *that* person for other women, no matter what their problems are."

I smiled sweetly, as though I had the situation all figured out. "This time, though, I'll make sure they work *for* me, not against me. If having bodyguards is the price I must pay to win your approval," I said, wincing inside, "then I'll pay it."

For a long moment, he said nothing, as though weighing the pros and cons of my proposal. "Are you sure?" he said at last, his deep frown indicating he found my sudden capitulation too good to be true. "This is going to be a permanent arrangement, not just a ploy to get you what you want right now."

I drew in a deep breath, steeling myself to agree to give up my privacy *forever*. "Yes, it will be permanent."

After a moment, he nodded. "All right, but I don't want you thinking you can take unnecessary risks just because you have protection. You come to me when you have questions or need advice. Understood?"

"Of course," I said happily, sealing our agreement with a deep, heartfelt kiss. "You're the only one I trust. I wouldn't dream of asking anyone else." I shrugged. "Who knows? My first case may come to nothing anyway. According to Ethel, the police ruled it an accident."

Will let out a deep sigh. "I'm glad that's settled. We should have hired a team to protect you a long time ago." He sounded relieved as his shoulders relaxed under my palms. Sliding his strong arms around me, he pulled me to his chest, pressing his mouth against mine. The deep passion in his kiss curled my toes.

"I know a few trustworthy guys who might be interested in the job," he murmured in my ear. "I'll contact them in the morning."

I laughed nervously, once again, feeling my freedom slip away. "Ah…why don't you hire one and I'll hire the other one? I should have a say in this, too."

Will didn't smile at the idea, but the worry in his eyes had softened. Breathing a silent sigh of relief, I rejoiced at gaining his approval. Now I just had to survive the fight ahead. And what a fight it would be, earning the respect of the public as the first female detective in the Twin Cities. It was a daunting concept, but one I accepted as I embarked on getting answers for Marjorie Kimball.

Ready or not, my new adventure was about to begin.

Chapter Three

Two days later, October 28th

The crisp morning air nipped at my nose, my breath billowing in a white mist as I hurried along the tree-lined boulevard to the red brick building on the busy southwest corner of Selby Avenue and Dale Street. Bright yellow leaves blanketed the sidewalk, adding a colorful glow to the sunny autumn morning. Ethel had made good on her word, securing a space for my office in a two-story building owned jointly by her and her husband, although Willard Rogers vigorously disagreed with her on that point. He didn't believe women were equal partners in anything, least of all business matters. But when Ethel found out that Will had agreed to my new business venture, she quickly secured space for my new office, making good on her promise to me. Regardless of Willard's views on women, it was obvious to me who wore the pants in *that* family.

The sign painter, a short, portly man with a beefy neck wearing a light blue cotton shirt, dark trousers with suspenders, and a newsboy cap, had arrived early and was busy putting the finishing touches on the glass portion of the door as I approached. I paused and stared with pride at the lettering, *C. E. Van Elsberg, Private Investigator*. It was official! Once Tri-State installed my telephone and I received my new number, I could get business cards printed and I would be ready to start taking clients.

My new office sat near the back stairway on the second floor. Formerly a storage room, the square space had a worn wooden floor, a noisy radiator, and a battered pebble-glass door, but to me, it was beautiful. My own little fiefdom. My heart swelled with exhilaration at the thought. I'd purchased new furniture and set up the delivery for today. I couldn't wait to put my professional house in order.

The painter began to pack up his equipment. "If yer husband is around, I'd like him to review the signage. If he approves, he owes me eight dollars."

I reached into my bag and pulled out a wad of bills, peeling off what he requested. "It's perfect," I said quickly, deciding not to tell him the sign was actually for me. After he got over his initial shock, he would probably insist that my husband approve the job anyway. "He's busy with a client this morning. He told me to handle this for him."

Giving me a surprised look, the man pocketed my money and began to pick up his equipment. "Tell yer husband, don't be touchin' those letters for a few days. She's dry to the finger by tomorrow, sure, but the paint's still soft. Give her a good week before you go washin' that glass, or you'll lift the paint clean off. Best to just let her sit and harden. She'll last years if you do."

I thanked him and went into my office, closing the door behind me.

As I entered the room, a strong odor of fresh paint assaulted my nostrils. Ethel had given Tom Stevens, the building manager, orders to paint the walls and clean the floors immediately. I placed my new attaché case with my initials stamped on the brown leather on the floor. I had purchased it to carry notes from my cases home with me.

I undid the buttons of my maroon cardigan sweater and slipped it off, along with my matching cloche hat. Folding the sweater neatly, I laid the items on top of my attaché case and wandered toward the single window in the back wall. It faced a small parking area for the renters and a stretch of the alley. Not much of a view…

A cool breeze rushed in, spreading goosebumps across my arms as I raised the window several inches to air out the room. I spun around and went to put my heavy wool sweater back on when the door swung open and Ethel Rogers appeared.

She wore a custom-made black, double-breasted suit with a straight skirt and a starched white blouse. "Good morning, Char!" The sharp lines on her face deepened when she smiled. "Welcome to your new office! It's a little small," she said, glancing around, "but it's the best I could do on short notice."

"It's absolutely fine, Ethel," I replied, buttoning up my sweater. "This is all I need to get started."

"Have you decided on a name for your firm yet?" Ethel asked, staring dubiously at the lettering on my door. "You need something that sounds business-like."

I looked around, wondering if my office looked professional enough to receive clients. "I've been so busy getting set up, I haven't really given it much thought yet. My furniture is being delivered this morning, and the phone company is installing my telephone tomorrow. I've already been to the print shop, and as soon as I get my new number, they'll print a few business cards."

"Good," Ethel stated happily as she scratched a spot of cream-colored wall paint off the door. "Then I'll set up the meeting with Marjorie for tomorrow afternoon. I need a little more time to convince her of the idea, anyway."

I blinked in surprise. "What do you mean?"

Ethel frowned and looked away. "She's not convinced that an independent investigation will do any good."

Her reply left me speechless. I stared at my name painted on the open door as a wave of shock washed over me. What was the point of going to all this trouble if Mrs. Kimball wasn't keen on the idea in the first place? Was it because she didn't have faith in a woman to get the truth?

Ethel's face flushed with embarrassment at my shocked reaction. "Don't worry about Marjorie," she assured me, patting my shoulder. "She's never had cause to hire an investigator before and questions whether the money is worth it, but I know she'll come around. She needs to know the truth of what happened to Eleanor."

The heavy clang of a vehicle door slamming interrupted us. I moved toward the window and peered down at the alley at a dark green truck with a wooden cargo box on the back. Two men jumped out. They walked toward the back and swung open the cargo doors. One wore dark brown pants and a cream shirt under a brown leather jacket. The other wore bib overalls and a blue plaid shirt under a thick gray sweater. Both wore flat caps. "The delivery truck is here from Sears, Roebuck and Company with my furniture."

"You're going to be busy for a while. I'd better be on my way and leave you to it," Ethel said hastily as she turned to leave. She paused in the doorway, however, as though she had something pressing on her mind. "Eleanor's funeral is this afternoon. I think we should go."

I didn't like the notion of showing up at a funeral to pay my respects when I had no connection to the deceased. Mrs. Kimball might think I'd come just to sell her on the idea of hiring me. The very notion troubled me.

"Don't worry, my dear," Ethel said as though reading my thoughts. "The crowd at the church will be huge, so it'll be easy for you to keep a low profile. I just think it would be good for you to see Eleanor and get a sense of who she was." She checked the diamond-encrusted timepiece on her wrist. "The service starts at two o'clock. I'll pick you up at home at one."

As soon as Ethel left, I went back to the window, opening it all the way. "You can bring the furniture up the back staircase," I called through the screen. "I'm right at the top of the stairs."

The two men stared curiously at me as though surprised to be taking orders from a woman. One man took off his brown, flat cap and ran his hand over his thinning hair. "We're delivering furniture for C. Van Elsberg," he said. "Is that your boss?"

"I'll come down and open the door for you," I answered abruptly, sidestepping his question. I didn't feel like explaining that the furniture was for me.

I ran downstairs and propped open the door as the men pulled my desk off the truck and carried it to the building. The older man nearly dropped his end of the piece and suddenly began berating the younger one. Somehow, it was the younger man's fault, even though as I watched them carry it into the building and up the stairs, I didn't see the younger one stumble or huff and puff as his partner did.

When they finally reached my office, I instructed them to place it close to the window. They were removing the twine that held the drawers in place when the younger one turned his back to me, revealing a long braid of dark hair, and I suddenly realized that he was actually a *she*.

"Take these off," the older one said and threw a piece of twine at her. "I need a smoke."

Ignoring me, he stomped out of the office. A moment later, his boots thundered on the wooden treads as he hurried down the back stairs.

"Don't pay him no mind," the woman said with an apologetic and deeply embarrassed smile at his rudeness. "Ray musta got up on the wrong side of the bed this morning."

I smiled back, wondering what she was doing working with a curmudgeon like Ray. She was tall and solidly built for a young woman in her early twenties. She had to be quite strong to carry my desk upstairs, and I wondered if she'd previously worked in a factory. "Is Ray your husband?"

Her warm brown eyes twinkled, the dimples in her round cheeks deepening as she burst out laughing. "No, ma'am. I'm not married, but if I were, I'd never pick him!"

"What's goin' on up there?" Ray hollered from the alley. "Al! Get down here and start carrying up these chairs!"

Al quickly finished pulling twine off the drawers and hurried downstairs.

I pulled a pad and pen from my attaché case and started jotting down a list of items that I needed for my office, such as an appointment diary, a calendar, and a desk blotter. And an electric percolator.

"Slow down!" Ray bellowed, his rough voice drifting through the window.

I stared through the screen, wincing as I watched him drop my wood and leather desk chair that he had pulled off the truck.

"Take it upstairs!" he snapped and turned his back on Al. "I'll get the lamps."

Al picked up the chair as if it were a pillow and carried it up to my office. I had two wingback chairs and two lamps still on the truck. I hoped they made it upstairs in one piece.

After Al arrived with my chair, I sat down and finished my list, adding a room-sized rug, a small bookcase, and a coat tree to my long, itemized account of needed supplies. I tried to ignore Ray and Al as they delivered the rest of my furniture, but the way that Ray barked orders and slung insults at Al, berating her for out-performing him in every respect, grated on my nerves.

I was still fuming about it long after they'd finished when suddenly, loud voices cut through the air. I spun around in my chair and peered through the window screen. Al stood in front of Ray, clutching a mewling kitten to her chest.

"You're not bringing that mangy cat along!" Ray yelled, glaring at her. "Put it back where you found it and get in the truck. We've got work to do!"

"Why not, Ray?" Al cried, her voice breaking with disappointment. "It ain't hurtin' nothin. It's all alone."

"'Cause it ain't our problem," Ray hollered. "Now do as I say, or I'll wring its neck. That meowing is irritatin' me."

Al clutched the tiny body to her chest with both hands as if to protect it from him. "It's just hungry. A little cream will quiet it."

"We ain't got time for that," he snapped as he slammed the doors shut on the back of the truck. "So, dump it and let's get going."

"No! I'm not leavin' it!"

Ray lunged for the cat, but Al quickly blocked him with her arm. Raising his hand to slap her, his face paled when she suddenly grabbed his shirt with one hand and lifted him off the ground. "Don't you lay a hand on it, Ray. This little thing never hurt nobody and doesn't deserve to be treated like yesterday's trash."

"You're fired, whore!" Ray roared, purple-faced with fury. "Find your own way home."

She set him down and backed away, watching as he jumped into the truck and drove away, leaving her in the alley clutching the mewling kitten to her chest.

Bolting from my chair, I raced downstairs and out the back door. "Are you all right?"

Tears ran down her face as she stroked the kitten. "I didn't mean to get rough with him. I just wanted him to leave this poor kitty alone. I'm sorry you had to see that."

"Don't let it get you down, kid," I said sympathetically and patted her shoulder. "That sap isn't worth it. He called you a whore!" Folding my arms into a tight bow, I stared down the alley where the truck drove off, still seething at his behavior. "When I heard him say that I was ready to come down here and clobber him myself. Who does he think he is?"

"That's my name," Al said with a loud sniff. "I'm Alice Horr, H-o-r-r."

"Well, you're really strong, Alice. Where did you learn how to defend yourself like that?"

"I grew up on a farm in North Dakota," Alice answered as she gently stroked the kitten. "I didn't have any brothers, so me and my sister had to share the farm work with my pa." She grinned. "We used to throw hundred-pound bales at each other when we got into a fight."

No wonder she was so strong. And good with animals. An idea began to percolate in my mind... "Do you know how to use a gun?"

"Sure," Alice replied proudly. "Me and Aggie used to go huntin' every fall with Pa. I can knock the spots off a ladybug at a hundred yards. I like to fish in the creek, too."

"Can you drive a vehicle?"

"Yes, ma'am. That's how I got the job workin' with Ray."

I looked her straight in the eye. "How would you like to work for me?"

She frowned. "Doin' what? A cook or a maid?" She shook her head. "I ain't no good at housework."

I laughed. "No. Nothing that dull. I want you to be my bodyguard."

"Me?" She stared at me as her brows knitted together with confusion. "Why would you need protection? Are you doin' something illegal?"

"Oh, no, nothing like that. I…I'm a woman of means," I said hesitantly, "and my husband is insisting that I hire bodyguards to accompany me wherever I go. You see…" I paused, not sure how to explain my new profession. "I'm also a private investigator."

It felt odd to say that about myself, but I needed to get used to it if I expected others to believe it as well.

"A lady investigator?" Her dark eyes lit up with admiration. "Well, I never… But, I don't…" She stared at her worn boots. "I'm just a dumb farm girl. I ain't the kind of person who'd fit in with a sophisticated lady like you. Besides, I don't have clothes for that kind of work. Don't own nothin' but these here overalls."

It distressed me to see how life had beaten her down. "Don't worry about your clothes," I said with an encouraging wave of my hand. "It'll be my pleasure to outfit you to fit the job. The way you handled Ray was impressive. You're tough and independent, with a heart for others in need. That's good enough for me. The job pays twenty-five dollars a week with room and board."

"All right, I guess I can give it a try," Alice said, staring at me as though she'd never imagined making that much money a week in her life. "My room rent is due tomorrow. When do you want me to start?"

"How about right now?"

The fluffy kitten began crying again.

"Aw, what a pretty little thing. It's a calico, isn't it? There's a corner grocery store across the street. Let's walk over there to get some cream," I said, checking my watch. It was only ten o'clock. Plenty of time to take Alice shopping for the proper clothes and get back home in time to change for the funeral.

After we filled the kitten's tummy, we came back to the building and went into Madeline's Salon, the cosmetics store on the first floor. The owner, Madeline Van Elsberg, coincidentally, was Will's sister and one of my best friends. I used Maddie's telephone to call home and tell Errol to pick us up. Then I bought Alice, much to her embarrassment, an assortment of lotions, hair and bath products, assuring her that it was a necessary part of her new position.

When Errol arrived, I introduced them and instructed him to take us to a department store where I bought Alice two men's-style suits, a smart-looking felt Fedora, stockings, underwear and shoes. Then we went to her boarding house to get her things. We arrived home just in time for me to introduce her to my staff and quickly change before Ethel's Packard limousine pulled into the carriage porch.

My goodness, my day had been busy. Was this what it was like to be an investigator? If so, I needed to get that appointment diary fast.

Chapter Four

Westminster Presbyterian Church

Minneapolis, Minnesota

I had doubts that attending Eleanor Kimball's funeral would provide any useful information about her death, but I kept those thoughts to myself. Ethel had gone to a lot of trouble to help me get this investigation started, and I couldn't disappoint her.

As our limousine approached the corner of Nicollet Avenue and Twelfth Street in downtown Minneapolis, the church loomed ahead, its twin limestone towers rising like solemn sentinels. In the past, I had driven by it a few times but never paid much attention to it. Today, I stared in awe at the grandeur of its rough-hewn walls and its centerpiece, a two-story, circular stained-glass window tinted deep rose.

Ethel hadn't exaggerated. Minneapolis's finest crowded the wide steps of Westminster Church to pay their respects. Gentlemen in tailored coats and homburg hats stood beside wives in sleek cloche hats and fox stoles, chatting about the symphony at the Shubert Theatre, partying at the Minneapolis Club, and exchanging gossip as though the funeral for Eleanor Kimball was as much of a social occasion as a solemn service. Perhaps it was simply a way to keep their spirits up, but it seemed to me as though saying goodbye to Eleanor had become as much of a society event as a sacred one.

I grew up attending a small Lutheran church on the east side of St. Paul, so the moment I stepped through the massive oak doors of

Westminster, the magnificence of the sanctuary overwhelmed me. The vaulted ceiling soared overhead, its dark wood beams reflecting the rose-colored light filtering through the huge stained-glass window. Rows of mahogany pews were already filled, the congregation's faces solemn, expectant. At the front, a polished wooden casket rested on a raised dais, surrounded by vases of lilies, carnations, and chrysanthemums in fall colors. Off to one side, dozens of bouquets of roses ranging from pristine white to deep crimson added a final, tender tribute.

A pair of ushers in black suits solemnly greeted us as we entered, offering Ethel and me each a printed funeral program. I opened mine and found a small portrait of Eleanor inside. A profound sense of sadness settled over me. It seemed so unfair that a woman so lovely and so young should already be gone.

"I knew the funeral would be well attended," Ethel murmured as we walked down the center aisle to get in line to view the deceased. "I just never expected it to be *this* huge." Raising her brows, she nodded discreetly toward a small group at the front of the church, quietly conversing. "My word. Even the governor is here."

The governor? I stared in awe. And at Ethel…good heavens. We'd only been friends for a few months, having met through our mutual interest in *Anna's House*, a women's shelter. I had no idea that she carried such weight in Minneapolis' elite society.

I shifted my gaze to the casket, careful not to reveal how this revelation had sent tremors through me. Until now, I hadn't grasped just who I was dealing with or how deeply the outcome of this case could impact my own reputation.

As the line moved along, Ethel greeted people she knew sitting in the pews, but she refrained from chatting to avoid having to introduce me. As for me, I buried my nose in my program and stayed close to her.

It seemed like an eternity before we reached the head of the line. Stepping toward the dais, my reaction took me by surprise. The casket, crafted from rich, polished cherrywood, looked exactly like the one I had selected nearly a year ago for my mother's funeral. It even had the same ornate, silver-plated handles and rich cream satin lining. And like back then, the heavy, cloying fragrance of fresh lilies hung in the air.

Eleanor rested in her casket, wearing a black chiffon gown with a white, crocheted collar. The moment I gazed upon her oval face framed by dark marcel waves and soft curls, I imagined that my own mother, Anna, might have looked similar at that age. Eleanor's slender hands were crossed over her chest, her large engagement ring catching the light as her fingers covered a small leather-bound Bible.

I stared at the small, worn New Testament, a poignant reminder of my mother's deep regard for her faith. I wasn't the kind of gal who cried at the drop of a hat, but suddenly, a wave of loneliness and despair overtook me, blurring my vision with tears. I swallowed hard, struggling to keep my composure, but the grief of losing her was too strong. Pulling an embroidered handkerchief from my pocket, I covered my mouth, trying desperately not to sob.

Ethel's hand rested gently on my arm, bringing me back to the present. "Are you all right?"

Her gentle, caring words brought fresh tears. I sniffled and shook my head, unable to speak.

A mature couple stood close to the casket, receiving people as they finished viewing the deceased. I didn't get a good look at them, but I reasoned they were Eleanor's parents. Turning away, I covered my mouth with my handkerchief again, hoping they wouldn't notice me.

An elderly gentleman in a clergy collar, tall and slim with white hair, approached me and took my hand. "Allow me to escort you to a quieter place," he whispered kindly. "Where you can gather your thoughts in prayer and have a glass of water."

Nodding, I allowed him to lead me out of the sanctuary to a small chapel near the front of the church, a narrow room with tall windows draped in heavy brocade curtains. An Oriental rug covered the polished oak floor, surrounded by a leather settee, fringed floor lamps, and small side tables. One table held a pitcher of water and a tray of glasses. The other held a clear vase of fresh flowers.

He poured a glass of water for me. "I'll let your companion know where she can find you."

"Thank you," I managed to squeak out as I sipped my water. "I appreciate your kindness."

As soon as he departed, I sat back and gulped my water, feeling like a silly fool. "Well, that was embarrassing," I whispered to myself, exhaling a deep breath. "I've managed to make a mess of my first task! Instead of keeping a low profile, I made such a fuss that everyone was looking at me!"

Ethel appeared in the doorway. "How are you feeling?"

"I'm fine," I said contritely. "I'm sorry for making such a spectacle of myself. Seeing Eleanor in that beautiful casket reminded me of my mother's funeral…"

"No harm done. We'll sit in the back so we can leave for the cemetery as soon as it's over," she said, getting back to business. "Are you feeling up to going back to the sanctuary now?"

I drained my water and stood, setting the empty glass on the tray. "Yes, let's go. By the way, did the Kimballs ask about me?"

Ethel shook her head. "No. When you left, they were speaking with Betty Britt. She's the mother of Eleanor's fiancé."

"Gosh, I hope Mr. and Mrs. Britt didn't notice my… unfortunate episode." I swallowed hard, wishing I hadn't made such a fool of myself.

"Betty's a widow," Ethel said bluntly. "Her husband died five years ago on a hunting trip. Dropped dead from a heart attack." She shook her head. "If you ask me, Betty and Marjorie looked tense enough to tear each other's hair out. I had no idea that they don't get along very well."

"That's a strange way to act at a funeral, especially for the mother of the deceased. I wonder what's really going on between those two," I remarked to myself as I followed her, making a mental note to jot that in my notebook and follow up on it later.

*　　*　　*

We sat through the service and quietly slipped out as soon as it ended. In the limousine on the way to the cemetery, I made a few notes in the notebook I stored in my attaché case. I'd brought the case along to add additional information to what I had so far, leaving it in the car while we were at the funeral.

I had two new avenues of pursuit. First, I wanted to know more about the relationship between Mrs. Kimball and Mrs. Britt. Second, I'd learned during the service that Eleanor belonged to a book discussion group that met twice a month. I needed to follow up on that and talk to those women.

But first, I needed to meet with the client. Was I on this case or not? It didn't make sense to begin interviewing people until I knew for sure that she wanted me to pursue this.

"Did you set up the meeting with Mrs. Kimball?" I asked Ethel.

She didn't answer. Instead, she stared ahead as though deep in thought. "Tomorrow afternoon," she suddenly blurted. "At three o'clock. I'll pick you up at two-thirty."

The way she forced out the words made me wonder if Marjorie Kimball had made up her mind yet or if Ethel was still trying to talk her into it. I sighed. Why did things always have to be so complicated?

At Lakewood cemetery, we stood in the back of the massive crowd. I wore a black cloche hat with a veil reaching my chin, which gave me the freedom to look about freely. When Ethel pointed out Matthew Britt, Eleanor's fiancé, I scrutinized him closely.

A muscular man of medium height, dressed in a black suit, with thick, curly blond hair and a thin, reddish mustache, Mr. Britt appeared to be about thirty. He stood close to the casket, his arm draped respectfully around his mother, yet there was something about him that unsettled me. He'd just lost the love of his life. There should have been deep pain in his eyes, but it wasn't there. There should have been sorrow etched across his face, yet only a mask of solemnity remained, so practiced that it bordered on boredom. Why? The question lodged in my mind, demanding an answer.

The minister began to read a psalm, but I couldn't concentrate on the service. I'd come here to glean everything I could about Eleanor's life, and that was what I intended to do. Scanning the crowd, I noticed a mature gentleman in a dark suit and hat standing alone, clutching a wrinkled handkerchief. His eyes were red from crying. His hands shook with distress as though he'd lost his best friend. Had he? Or…was he a close relative who simply wanted to grieve alone?

I nudged Ethel with my elbow. "Who is that?"

She frowned at me through her veil of fine black netting. "My dear, there are at least two hundred people at this service," she whispered. "I can't tell who you're looking at."

"Over there," I insisted with a slight jerk of my head. "That man. The older gentleman standing by the maple tree."

Ethel glanced at him, then looked away. "I don't know him. Why?"

"He's having a difficult time getting through the service."

Ethel looked again. "He's probably a close relative of the family."

But something about his grieving bothered me. It seemed too deep, too personal as though his heart was irrevocably broken. I looked away, wondering how he knew Eleanor. Once the service ended, I intended to ask him. After a few moments, I glanced past my shoulder again.

"He must have realized we were watching him," I whispered in disappointment. "He's gone."

Ethel checked her wristwatch. "I think it's about time for us to leave, too. When this thing ends, the traffic jam in this place is going to be horrendous, and I've got another engagement in about an hour." She pointed toward a curved road going up a wooded hill. "My driver said he'd park the car somewhere over there. If we hurry, we can get out of here before the crowd disperses."

We left the service and made our way up the hill to locate the car. Within minutes, we were on our way home. Settling comfortably in my seat, I pulled out my notebook and began scribbling my thoughts about the mysterious man who didn't want his presence noticed. Was he the missing driver who crashed Eleanor's car and left her for dead?

I needed to find out.

Chapter Five

By the time Ethel dropped me off at home, I was exhausted and needed a nap. The trouble was, I had barely an hour to change for dinner and spend a few precious minutes with my children. I always spent time with them every night before they went to bed.

Gerard, my English butler, opened the front door the instant I reached it. "Good evening, My Lady," he said with a slight bow. His deep, resonant voice carried a theatrical quality, as though delivering a line in a play. If he ever chose to pursue acting, Shakespeare would suit him perfectly.

A stout man in his mid-fifties, Gerard had dark wavy hair, brown eyes, impeccable grooming, and *very* stately manners. He had immigrated to America from England several years ago and had been working for me since last April. I loved the deep, melodious rumble of his voice and the formality of his British accent when he called me "*My Lady*."

"Good evening, Gerard." Ripping off my hat, I handed it to him along with my case, instructing him to set the case in the library.

"Cook has advised me that Miss Francie is attending the pictures tonight with a friend to see the movie *Son of the Sheik* starring Rudolph Valentino," Gerard said, his usual stoic manner softening to almost a smile, relieved no doubt to be spared the duty of keeping my headstrong sixteen-year-old sister off the telephone when she was supposed to be doing her studies.

If both Will and I were out, Francie needed our cook's permission to go out with her friends. From the day she was hired, our cook, Adelaide, made it clear everyone was to address her as *Cook* to establish her authority in the kitchen, and she had earned our respect many times over. I trusted Cook's judgment without reservation, especially where Francie was concerned. I'd promised my mother on her deathbed that I'd take good care of Francie, and I intended to keep my word.

"Mr. Van Elsberg is in the den with your new bodyguard," Gerard said. "He's requested that you join him as soon as you arrive."

Pleased that Will had already met Alice, I followed Gerard through the library into the den, a long, narrow room that Will had converted into an office. Will sat at his desk, conversing with another man sitting across from him in one of the visitor chairs. They both stood as I entered.

"Hello, darling," Will said, kissing me on the cheek. "I'd like to introduce you to Sean McBride. He'll be the lead guard on your new security team." He turned to Sean. "Sean, this is my wife, Char."

"Hello," Sean said in a clear, deep voice as he extended his broad hand. He loomed above me—but then, at five feet, two inches tall, most people did. It wasn't just his height, however, that caught my attention. He had dark hair swept back, sharp gray eyes, and a thick black mustache. His dark suit and crisp white shirt added to his air of authority.

"Hello, Sean. I'm pleased to meet you," I said, stunned by Will's words. The lead guard... Wasn't it up to me to decide that? I had expected both of my bodyguards to be equal, but the easy way that Will referred to Sean taking the lead over my security gave me the feeling he had instructed Sean to keep him informed of my activities. I shook hands with the man, sensing my autonomy slip away, and it unsettled me. My bodyguards answered *to me* and no one else. I was not going to be led around on a leash again by guards who only took orders from my husband, and that was *that*.

"I've invited Sean to dine with us tonight to give you a chance to get to know him before you start working together," Will said with a smile.

Oh, did you? I thought disappointedly. I had hoped for a quiet meal with Will to talk about my case, but that obviously wasn't going to happen now.

"I'd like you to meet the other half of the team," I said briskly, deciding that if Sean was going to dine with us, then Alice was too. "I'll be right back."

I left the den and passed through the library into the large reception hall we called the great hall. The two-story, hundred-foot room, embellished with hand-carved oak woodwork and cut-glass chandeliers, was the centerpiece of our home. Will and I were married here. To my right, the grand staircase, flanked by thick Doric columns, led up to a wide landing where it divided into two staircases, one to the right and one to the left, both leading to the second floor. Multiple windows with etched glass spread across the back wall, filling the airy space with soft, natural light.

I crossed the great hall to the back stairs that led to the servant's quarters. By chance, I met Alice coming towards me.

"They said you was home, Miz Char," she announced with a smile. "I just wanted to thank you for these new clothes. I ain't never had anything this nice before."

"They look absolutely smashing on you," I replied, taking in her new outfit. She wore a navy pinstriped suit, double-breasted with men's trousers and a silky white bow blouse. "Alice, you're the bee's knees!"

Alice's face flushed at the compliment, but it pleased me to see her laugh. "What is the name of your agency?" she asked curiously.

"I don't know," I replied slowly. "I'm still thinking about it."

"Can I help?"

"Sure. I'm open to suggestions. Now, come with me," I said warmly. "I'd like to introduce your partner. He's in the den with Will."

I led Alice into the den and nearly burst out laughing at the men's reactions. Will's jaw dropped the moment he saw her, while Sean stared at her as though I'd mistakenly brought in the cleaning lady. So, they were shocked by my choice of bodyguard. Well, they'd better get used to it because Alice wasn't going anywhere but with me.

"Gentlemen, meet Alice Horr," I said proudly. "From now on, wherever I go, she goes."

Will finally remembered his manners and reached out to shake her hand. "It's nice to…er…meet you," he said, nervously clearing his throat. "Welcome to our home. I trust our staff has been helpful in getting you settled in?"

"Yes, sir," Alice replied shyly, staring at the floor.

Sean glared at Will. "What's this? You didn't tell me I'd be working alongside *a woman*. I signed up to protect *her*," he complained, pointing at me, then at Alice. "Not play nursemaid to *her*."

"Nobody needs to be my nanny," Alice spouted indignantly. "I can take care of myself. And Miz Char!"

"Alice is my choice," I said brazenly to Sean. "You are Will's. If it bruises your ego to work with a couple of strong women, then perhaps you aren't—"

"I'm up to the job," Sean burst out, his face turning red with indignation. "And she'd better be, too, 'cause I'm not working with someone who doesn't pull his weight!"

Alice started to protest when Will cleared his throat, indicating he wanted to change the subject. "Let's have a drink, shall we?" Reaching down, he pulled a bottle of bootlegged whiskey from his desk and several glasses. He winked at me. "I keep a bottle of good whisky on hand—purely for medicinal purposes, you understand."

I almost laughed. Yes, we all needed to calm down, especially me. I didn't like Sean, but he was Will's choice, so I needed to set my feelings aside and work with him. "None for me," I said, indicating that Will should give my glass to Alice instead. "I never touch the stuff."

"Thank you." Alice accepted her drink and tossed it back like water. "Jeepers, that's some mighty fine hooch," she said without so much as a blink of the eye, setting the glass on the desk. "Much better than my pa used to make."

I looked at the clock. Dinner was only forty-five minutes away. "If you'll excuse me, I need to get ready for dinner."

Alice and I left the den together. We parted ways at the grand staircase but agreed to meet in the dining room at seven o'clock. I said goodbye and rushed upstairs.

Lillian, my personal maid, had spread out a beaded amethyst drop-waist dress with a V-neck on the bed and had already drawn my bath. I bathed, changed into the chiffon gown, and sat at my lighted dressing table while she touched up my hair.

"How was your day, my lady? You look a bit tired," Lillian asked softly as she restyled my hair. She and I were about the same age, but that was where our similarities ended. She was tall and willowy, compared to my petite, five-foot, two-inch frame. She had light brown hair, amber-colored eyes, and a very pale complexion. I wore my dark hair chin-length, parted on the side, framed with soft waves and spit curls. I loved to wear red lipstick.

"Yes, I am tired," I replied, unable to stifle a yawn. "I've been rushing since breakfast."

Her slender hands stilled above my head. "Will you be retiring early then? Would you like me to turn down the bed right away?"

I shook my head. I could easily have slid into bed right now and slept like a rock all night, but then I'd miss dinner and spending time with my children. "The usual time will be fine."

I arrived at the nursery on the third floor with fifteen minutes to spare and found my nanny at the changing table readying Nora for bed. Eleven-month-old Julien stood beside the settee in his nightgown, gripping it to keep his balance. His eyes lit up the moment he spotted me. He laughed, pounding his chubby hand on the cushion while a ribbon of drool slipped between his front teeth cascading down his flannel bib. My heart swelled to behold my sweet little man.

"Come to Mamma," I whispered softly and held out my arms. He lifted one hand to reach me as I knelt and picked him up. "My goodness, you're getting so big I can hardly lift you."

The spitting image of my late husband, Gus, Julien was tall for his age with sandy-colored curls and eyes beginning to take on the same grayish green as his father's. Sometimes I felt sad that Gus had died before his only child was born, but Gus had lived a dangerous life as a bootlegger and his death had been as volatile as his life.

I sat on the settee with Julien on my lap and held him close, praying that the world he grew up in would be kinder than the one Gus had left behind.

Chapter Six

October 29th

"Last night went well," Will commented the next morning as we lingered over strong black coffee in the breakfast room. Golden sunlight filtered through the tall windows from the sun streaming between the mature oaks on the edge of our property. "Sean and Alice seemed to get along fine. What do you think?"

Sean's manners had come across as overly polite compared to his outburst in the den and I suspected that he was playing to an audience of one. The real test would come when Alice and I were alone with him. Would he be respectful or try to boss us around? I had my doubts about the former.

"I think I need to let them two sort it out and get going on my investigation," I replied staring into my glass of fresh-squeezed orange juice. "The truth is, I don't know where to start."

"Get to know your victim," Will offered. "Learn everything you can about her—where she lived, her friends and relatives, the places she liked to frequent. The information will provide valuable clues about her life and possibly reveal why she was killed."

Will set down his cup and leaned back as Gerard approached the table and placed a plate of scrambled eggs, bacon and toast in front of him. Will looked at me curiously. "You said she was engaged?" He paused to grab a bottle of Heinz Tomato Ketchup.

From the corner of my eye, I caught Gerard wincing at the idea of smothering one's eggs with that vile concoction. I agreed but kept my opinion to myself. Will loved ketchup, especially this brand, and poured it on his breakfast nearly every morning.

"Take a good look at her fiancé," Will said seriously. He shook the bottle, poring ketchup all over his eggs and filling the air with a pungent tomato aroma. "In my experience, when you're investigating the murder of a woman, the guilty party is quite often someone close to the victim. That doesn't make the fiancé automatically guilty, but it does make him a primary suspect until your investigation proves otherwise."

"Okay," I said, jotting down his instructions in my journal as Gerard set a plate of poached eggs and toast in front of me. Interviewing everyone who knew the deceased would be a huge undertaking. Was I up to the task? More importantly, would I gain anything useful from it? The thought exhausted me, and I hadn't started yet.

"Go back to the scene of the crime," Will continued and scooped up a forkful of eggs. "Study it, leaving no stone unturned. No detail is too small. Sometimes I find evidence that the police missed."

I picked up a slice of toast and concentrated on smothering it with Welch's Grape Jelly to avoid watching Will eat his *red* eggs. "Is there anything else I should know?"

"Read the autopsy report," he added as he picked up a crisp piece of bacon with his fingers. "The family might have requested their private physician to look it over and interpret it for them but unless they knew medical terms they wouldn't have a copy of it themselves. You need to grease a palm or two at the coroner's office to obtain a look at it."

Oh sure, I'll just drive to downtown Minneapolis and find someone in the coroner's office to give me a look-see at that report.

I let out a sigh and took a bite of my toast, pondering how I would actually go about getting someone in the coroner's office to give me access to the report, much less interpret it for me. I had no idea. "Do I need to read the autopsy report? Is it imperative to my case?"

"It's another piece of the puzzle, darling," Will said, his voice softening at my frustration. "If the police ruled her death an accident, the family would want to know if she'd suffered a medical issue at the time, causing her to lose control of the car. If there is a report, you should find out what's in it."

Folding my arms, I sat back and stared at him as discouragement began to seep into my mood. Had I made a mistake wanting to become an investigator? The job was clearly more than I'd bargained for.

He grabbed my hand and leaned close, kissing my cheek. "I'll do it for you. I've got a trustworthy contact there who'll come through for me. Is that okay?"

A huge burden had suddenly lifted off my shoulders. I smiled in appreciation, my enthusiasm reinvigorated. "That's a swell idea! Thank you, Will. You'll have to introduce me to your contact so in the future, I can approach him myself."

His smile faded. "We'll see. One step at a time."

What caused his reluctance? Did he expect me to get so discouraged with the process that I lost interest and changed my mind? Ethel was right. Will was my husband, my mentor and the key to becoming a *good* investigator. I needed to stop wallowing in my inexperience and tap his expertise as much as possible.

My discouragement faded, giving way to a sudden burst of energy. I had no intention of throwing in the towel. *I had work to do.* The next step was my meeting this afternoon with Mrs. Kimball, and then I intended to hit the trail at full speed.

*   *   *

Ethel's limousine glided into the carriage porch at precisely two-thirty. Ignoring Sean's objections over being left behind, I hurried down the front steps and climbed in alone. I doubted Ethel would welcome a pair of bodyguards trailing her like a posse, and I wasn't about to impose them on her. Besides, I needed to stay invisible at the funeral. Arriving with a pair of bodyguards in tow would attract a lot of attention and pull the focus away from where it rightly belonged—on Eleanor Kimball.

"Is there anything special I need to know about the Kimball family?" I asked Ethel once we were on our way to Minneapolis.

"They're an odd pair," Ethel remarked in a wry tone. "Marjorie frets endlessly about her social standing. She serves on a half-dozen charity boards and plays patron of the arts. As for Robert..." She raised one brow. "He's a banker who dabbles in the stock market and hobnobs with his friends at the country club. When he's not increasing his wealth, rumor has it there's a certain chorus girl that he's rumored to be carrying on with—right under Marjorie's nose."

"It doesn't sound like a happy marriage," I replied bluntly.

Ethel snorted, her countenance turning to stone. "The rich don't marry for love."

I pondered that for a while as I stared out the window, uneasy. Was she talking about the Kimballs—or her own life?

When we pulled up to the Kimball residence, I started to get a sense of what Ethel meant by marrying for money and status. This place reminded me of a castle. Nestled next to lush parkland with colorful perennial gardens, the stately dwelling was constructed of pale gray limestone that gleamed softly in the sunlight. A red slate roof sloped gracefully over the structure, punctuated by tall, arched windows and wide chimneys.

Wide steps led to a stone terrace at the front entrance, bordered by neatly manicured gardens and decorative wrought iron railings. Mature trees dotted the yard, their branches providing shade along the curved path that wound toward Lake of the Isles.

A male servant in a dark tailcoat with brass buttons welcomed us at the arched, wrought iron and glass doors, ushering us into a wide, marble-tiled foyer.

"Marjorie is expecting me, James," Ethel said to him, her tone cool and assured.

James led us to the sitting room, a cozy space with neutral walls, Persian rugs over hardwood floors, and southern-facing windows that offered sweeping views of the crystal blue lake. We settled on a settee of cream damask in front of a low, circular mahogany table. Side tables held fringed lamps in blue fabric, vases, and small sculptures. The furnishings were tasteful and well chosen, but the room lacked a personal touch, as though it had been designed by a professional rather than Mrs. Kimball herself.

After a short wait, Mrs. Kimball swept into the room with a practiced flourish like a glamorous film star, radiating elegance in a rose-colored silk crepe dress skimming her tall, slender frame. Her blonde-tinted bob gleamed under the chandelier, each finger-waved curve perfectly set in the latest Parisian style. Diamond-studded drop earrings caught the light and sparkled with each step.

"Marjorie," Ethel said dramatically as we both rose from the settee. She planted a kiss on the woman's cheek as though they were old friends. "I've brought someone for you to meet." She turned to me. "This is my friend, Charlotte Van Elsberg."

Marjorie's red lips puckered in confusion. "Who?"

"Charlotte," Ethel persisted. "The woman I told you could look into Eleanor's accident. She's a private investigator."

Marjorie's face suddenly paled as though she struggled to keep the pain of Eleanor's death from overwhelming her. After a moment, she tentatively held out her hand. "I—I'm pleased to meet you…"

A golden-skinned female servant wearing a black dress with a crisp white apron appeared out of nowhere. "Shall I serve refreshments, Mrs. Kimball?"

"That won't be necessary, Ivory," Marjorie replied to the black woman with a dismissive wave of her hand. "We won't be long."

"Yes, Ma'am," Ivory said, inclining her head, and disappeared as quietly as she appeared.

Ethel stiffened, clearly taken aback by Marjorie's colossal

display of rudeness.

"Would you like to visit the gardens?" Marjorie asked pivoting from the door as a passing figure cast a shadow across the floor. With a sharp tilt of her head, she frowned, projecting a silent warning. "It's such a beautiful day, and there is so little time left to enjoy the fall weather."

"I'd love to." Ethel nodded back, as though catching the subtle message. She snatched her beaded purse off the mahogany table and signaled to me to follow.

James stood like a sentinel at the front door as we stepped outside, descending the wide stone steps past urns overflowing with bright yellow and orange Chrysanthemums to a shady garden on the side of the house.

"Robert can't know about this," Marjorie said in a low, cautious tone. "He believes Eleanor's death was an accident and he considers the matter closed. Any attempt to dig up new information will cause doubt and suspicion, casting a blight on our reputation."

"I can be very discreet," I assured her. "Besides, a woman asking questions isn't going to cause concern like it would if a man began poking around."

Marjorie scrutinized me with a critical eye. "If I decide to retain your services, what assurances do I have that you're trustworthy? I've never heard of you. Are you affiliated with Pinkerton?"

"No, but I do have experience in handling all manner of issues, and I have great counsel," I replied, wishing I'd already chosen a name for my agency. At times like this, having an official-sounding name made me appear more professional. "My husband is also a private detective. His reputation is impeccable."

Marjorie's amber eyes lit up with curiosity. "Is that so? Perhaps I should hire him."

"He's overloaded with cases right now," Ethel said, injecting herself into the conversation. "He shares an office with an attorney, Peter Garrett, and he works almost exclusively with Peter's clients. Willard has needed their services a few times with real estate deals."

"But can a woman be as effective?" Marjorie asked, her eyes shadowed with lingering doubt.

Keeping my expression neutral, I refused to let my disappointment show. I'd expected men to doubt my competence, but not another woman. "I will get answers for you," I said firmly, my voice steady with resolve. "Give me a week. If I haven't reached a breakthrough by then, our agreement is off, and you owe me nothing. Fair enough?"

A tall, gray-haired man wearing a dark tweed suit appeared in the window, scrutinizing us with narrowed eyes.

"What a wonderful garden you have, Marjorie," Ethel said loudly and turned her back to the window.

Marjorie glanced back at the window and turned away quickly as well, confirming to me that the man in question was her husband, Robert. "My gardener came highly recommended," she replied in a nervous, high-pitched voice. "You'll have to come back in April when my spring perennials are in full bloom. Perhaps we'll have luncheon, then, too."

Ethel smiled conspiratorially as the three of us made our way toward her black limousine. "So, the agenda is set then? Charlotte will meet with you again in a few days to go over the specifics of the garden club's next outing."

Marjorie held off answering until we reached the car and out of the earshot of her husband. "All right," she said to me. "I'll meet with you again a week from today, but at nine o'clock when Robert is golfing. In the meantime, you are not to call my house under any circumstances. Is that clear? Robert must not get wind of what I'm doing, or he'll be upset."

"Yes, I understand," I replied with a nod. "I'll meet you here next Thursday at nine o'clock to give you all of the information I've acquired."

Marjorie engulfed Ethel with a hug. "Have a safe drive home."

I slid into the car with sweaty palms and a stomach churning with anxiety as Marjorie walked swiftly toward the house. I'd just promised to give her the information she so desperately needed in seven days. What possessed me to make such an outrageous claim?

I didn't care about the money. I had exactly one week to prove I was worth the trust she'd placed in me—or be finished as an investigator.

Chapter Seven

The moment Ethel's chauffeur shut the car door on us, the door on the other side opened and the woman Marjorie had referred to as Ivory slid in on the opposite seat, turning away from the window. She'd removed her white apron, revealing a solid black dress. She must have come around the opposite side of the house, concealing her presence by the trees and bushes.

"There's something you need to know," she said in a rush. "I can't be gone long, but I can spare a few minutes before anyone misses me. You can drop me off a couple of blocks from here, and I'll walk back to the house."

Ethel slid open the glass partition and spoke to her chauffeur, instructing him to drive to the filling station two blocks away.

Ivory looked to be in her mid-twenties with delicate features and flawless skin the shade of coffee, richly blended with cream. She wore her short ebony hair parted on the side with finger waves and cut in a style that closely matched Eleanor's. Slim and graceful, she carried herself with the poise of a ballerina.

The moment our car pulled out of the driveway, she began to speak. "Mrs. Kimball does want to know the truth of Miss Eleanor's death, no matter what you find." She glanced back at the house, her hands tightening into fists as we drove away. "It's *Mr.* Kimball who's totally against it. That's why Mrs. Kimball wants to keep things secret. If he got wind of what you are doing, he'd fire you immediately and cut off her household allowance—or worse." She let out a tense breath. "He can get ugly."

Ethel and I exchanged curious glances. That explained why Marjorie became so nervous when his shadow appeared in the window. I turned to Ivory. "I assure you, I will be discreet, but why do you think he's so against an investigation to confirm that it was truly an accident? You'd think he'd want to know!"

Ivory glanced from Ethel to me. "If Eleanor's death is the result of foul play, it would cause a scandal."

"Lordy, we can't have that," Ethel said sarcastically as she rolled her eyes. "Heaven knows that would create a lot of gossip, and all that man cares about is his reputation."

"That's why he pushed Miss Eleanor to accept Mr. Britt's proposal," Ivory said, leaning forward. "Matthew Britt's late father was an ambassador, and the family still has ties to many of Washington's elite. But you also need to know that the engagement between Miss Eleanor and Mr. Britt wasn't a match made in heaven. It wasn't much of a match at all. They fought all the time. If you want to find out what really happened to her, start with him."

Her boldness to speak out impressed me. "How do you know that her death looks suspicious?"

"We've heard things," she said with a shrug. "The staff is aware of everything that goes on in the Kimball house."

I should have realized that right away. My staff knew a lot more than I gave them credit for as well.

Ethel and I both spoke at once, but I managed to get my question out first. "Do you know what they fought about?"

Ivory chortled. "Money. Isn't that what every rich couple fights about? Miss Eleanor's family is loaded to the gills. They employ a large staff, and we get paid on time every week. That's not the case with the Britts." Her eyes narrowed in disgust. "I've gotten to know some of their staff, and the gossip is that Mr. Britt has gone through most of his late father's fortune. Because of their money issues, they often pay their staff late." She lifted one brow. "Sometimes not at all. Mr. Britt seems to find the money, though, to drink and play cards, but the gossip is that he's lousy at both. He needed Miss Eleanor's money to pay his debts. Miss Eleanor, or rather her parents, wanted the social clout that being related to the Britts would bring."

Ethel burst out with a wry laugh. "Dining with senators and their wives. Invitations to exclusive events. Marjorie would be on top of the world."

So that was why it surprised Ethel to see the governor at Eleanor's funeral. He'd come to show support for the Britt family on the loss of their future daughter-in-law. He likely hadn't met the Kimballs before that day.

"What's going on between Marjorie and Betty Britt?" Ethel blurted out. "I noticed some friction between them at the funeral. They were doing their best to be polite, but it was clear to me they don't like each other."

Ivory burst into a knowing smile, leaving me awestruck at how beautiful and well-spoken she appeared. With so much going for her, I wondered how she ended up working as a domestic servant. It was none of my business, of course, and I kept that question to myself.

"Mrs. Britt wants Miss Eleanor's engagement ring back," Ivory said boldly.

Ethel gasped. "The nerve of that woman! I'd be hostile to her too. The ring belongs to Eleanor's family now, and it's not Betty's to repossess."

"She claims that it's a family heirloom, so the Kimballs have no right to keep it. Supposedly, it's Grandma Britt's wedding ring. It's over two carats."

"Did they bury it with her?" I asked, speaking up.

Ivory shook her head. "The family had it removed, of course, before the hearse took Miss Eleanor's casket to the cemetery. Mrs. Kimball is well aware that it's a very expensive piece, but her reason for wanting to keep it is because it was a gift to Miss Eleanor, and she treasured it."

"And probably because it irks Betty to high heaven," Ethel remarked with a smirk. "Lord help me if I had to put up with that woman. I'd be tempted to put arsenic in her tea!"

Everyone laughed, lightening their mood.

The limousine pulled into a busy Standard Oil filling station where touring cars, sedans, and Model Ts idled as they waited in line to have their tanks filled and their windshields polished by uniformed attendants in caps and coveralls.

As Ivory threw open the door, the pungent scents of fresh gasoline and hot exhaust wafted into the car along with the rumble of idling engines. "I hope you find out who was in that car with her," Ivory said. "If I hear anything more, I'll let you know."

Wondering how she learned that detail, I handed her my card with my office number on it and my home telephone number handwritten on the back and thanked her for the information. Then suddenly, the door slammed shut, and she was gone.

* * *

When I arrived home, Will met me at the front door, instead of Gerard, and the grave look on his face indicated he wasn't pleased with me.

"Sean tells me that you went out today and left him home," he said in a gruff voice as I stepped into the wide front entryway. "If you're not going to abide by our agreement, then—"

"Oh, so Sean snitches on me every chance he gets, does he?" Incensed that my judgement was being questioned, I ripped off my hat and slammed it on the marble-topped side table for Gerard to retrieve. "Ethel took me in her limousine to meet Marjorie Kimball. It was a social call. There was no purpose in bringing along bodyguards. I went to assure her that I would uncover the true circumstances of Eleanor's death. Not intimidate her!"

"All right," Will said, softening his voice as he helped me slip out of my sweater. "Calm down. I guess I should have found out more about the situation before becoming concerned."

"I guess Sean should have been more forthcoming," I replied, toning down my anger. "You could have spoken to Alice about it. She would have told you where I went and why."

Will dropped my sweater on the table and pulled me into his arms. "Let's not argue, okay? I just want to have a nice quiet evening with my best gal."

Surprised, I looked into his deep blue eyes. "What other gals do you have?"

He smiled mischievously. "Let's see, she's a spunky little thing with dark hair and a loud roar when she gets angry. She's not shy about demanding attention."

I laughed. "And she has you wrapped right around her tiny finger, doesn't she?" Nora Rose had each of us dancing to her tune, and we both knew it.

Will tightened his arms around my waist and placed a tender kiss on my lips. "Did you have a productive day?"

"Oh, yes," I said and pulled him into the library, shutting the door behind us. "Outwardly, the Kimballs appear to be a unified couple, but behind closed doors, it's a different story. I think her husband, Robert, bullies her."

"Is that so?"

"Yes, unfortunately," I replied as he pulled me close again. "Marjorie Kimball made me swear that I'd keep my investigation secret because as she put it, if her husband found out she'd hired me behind his back he'd be upset."

Will pulled back staring at me with concern. "Is he a violent man?

Are you safe around him?"

"I don't know but I don't plan to be in the same house as him. Our next meeting will be when he's playing golf. She's expecting me to have some answers."

Nervous about placing a deadline on my investigation without knowing if I could meet it, I closed my eyes and let out a deep sigh. "Tomorrow I'm going to visit the place where the car ran off the road."

We were interrupted by the deep familiar rumble of someone clearing his throat followed by a sharp rap on the door. I opened it to find just who I expected—Gerard.

"Cook has given Miss Francie permission to dine with friends tonight. Will you be having any guests?" It was his tactful way of asking whether Sean and Alice would be joining us again.

"No," I replied determined to have my husband all to myself for one evening. "Dinner will be for two, Will and me."

He gave a slight bow. "Very good, My Lady. I'll pass the information along to Cook."

My sister could be a handful—always insisting on getting her way and determined to have the last word in every argument. I loved Francie dearly, but her stubbornness and willfulness were often the bane of my existence. Cook was strict but fair, handling Francie with patience. I trusted her judgment and was grateful to be able to rely on her.

I needed a quiet evening to collect my thoughts about tomorrow. Besides visiting the scene of the crash, I wanted to pay a visit to Betty Britt. The problem with that was, I couldn't reveal that I was investigating Eleanor's death. I had to come up with a believable cover by tomorrow and it had to be good. What excuse could I offer?

One slip, one word reaching Robert, and the investigation—and my career—would be over before it started.

Chapter Eight

October 30th

"Why aren't we taking the limousine?" Sean bellowed as we faced off in the garage the next morning. "It's bulletproof."

Errol, my chauffeur, stood off to the side in his overalls wiping his hands on a rag as he silently watched the scene unfold. Beside me, Alice planted her hands on her hips, giving Sean a silent glare. The flat, rectangular outline of a Smith and Wesson revolver I'd taken from Gus' gun collection bulged under her coat.

Sean gestured toward a black Model T hardtop that I had instructed him to drive. "This Tin Lizzie won't protect us from a hailstorm much less a hail of bullets. Either we're taking the limo or we're not going!"

Three days—two arguments. It hadn't taken this guy long to grate heavily on my nerves. First, he didn't like my choice of a female for his partner and now, he didn't like my choice of vehicles. I had absolutely no time for his theatrics.

"First off," I snapped, "no one is going to shoot at me. I'm not a bootlegger and never was. That was my late husband's world. Not mine. And everyone in the business knows I've walked away from it so I'm no threat to them. Second, an armored limousine with armed bodyguards in the front seat makes me look like a criminal who needs protection from her enemies. I'm trying to connect with people to solve a case, not intimidate them!"

I placed my hand on the car. "This is a brand-new hardtop. It came from the Ford dealership on West Seventh that *I* own thanks to my late husband Gus. It's a good car and we're using it so let's get going." I looked up to see Sean glowering at me. "And for your information, I know how to drive it so if you decide to sit this one out and pout, Alice and I can manage without you."

Alice looked away, struggling to muffle a small snicker.

Sean stomped toward the car and jerked the driver's side door open. "Fine, but Will's going to hear about this!"

Alice opened my door and stretched out her hand to assist me onto the back seat. "Up you go, Miz Char."

Oh, yes, was Will *ever* going to hear about this…

* * *

Before I set out for the day with my team, I'd placed a quick call to Ethel to find out when Eleanor became engaged and then had Sean drive me straight to the library to find a back issue of the Minneapolis paper. I needed to read the engagement announcement to get as much information as I could about the lovebirds. According to Ethel, the article was long and boring. And she was right, but it contained a mountain of valuable information about both people. Armed with this new knowledge, I had a good idea of how I planned to portray myself to people I needed to interview.

I'd also located an article about Eleanor's accident while I was there. According to the reporter, her car had veered off the road on a foggy evening a week ago. That day had been unusually warm and humid, leading to heavy fog at sunset.

I planned to stop and buy a map of the city to look up the accident location, but Sean knew of the place that the article had named. Once we reached the area, he drove south on Kenwood Parkway to "Millionaire's Row," where the road bent sharply near the northwest angle of Lake of the Isles at Mount Curve Avenue. There, the hill rose gently to the west, dotted with stately mansions, surrounded by luscious green lawns, and bordered with hedges and stone walls.

According to the engagement notice, the Britt family lived on Mount Curve Avenue. My, what a coincidence. Was Matthew Britt the unidentified person in Eleanor's car that fateful night?

The pavement gradually narrowed, becoming uneven with old, bumpy patches of tar showing where winter frost of past seasons had cracked the surface. The skeletal forms of mature, arching elms and maples lined the roadside, their dark trunks forming a shadowed wall as the turn approached. Beyond the bare trees, the lake gleamed in the morning light, its clear blue surface smooth and serene.

The sharp bend came suddenly, masked by a thick line of trees. There, the road sloped along a shallow embankment. Sean slowed the car and proceeded cautiously. At the same time, I noted the narrow shoulder, imagining how a car's tires might spin on wet leaves or loose gravel. Even in broad daylight, the curve demanded careful handling. At night, especially with dense fog, it would be treacherous.

We all saw the tire marks veering off the road at the same time and spoke at once. "There it is!"

Sean pulled to the side of the road and quickly jumped out. He opened my door, extending his hand to help me climb down. Alice got out and joined us to inspect the scene. The wheels of Eleanor's vehicle had made ruts in the wet ground where it drove off the road in a straight line, rolled down a shallow embankment and ended at the trunk of a huge elm tree.

"It looks like she didn't see the curve," Sean pointed out.

"And she was going pretty fast by the deep chunk of bark taken out of that tree," Alice added as she pointed to a huge notch in the tree where the bumper must have crashed into it.

I canvassed the area, hoping to find more clues. To my disappointment, the thick blanket of leaves covering the moist ground had made it impossible to see footprints, but something else caught my attention.

"Look at this," I said pointing to a cigarette butt next to my foot where my shoe had dislodged a small mound of leaves.

Sean swooped down and picked it up. "It's a Turkish smoke." He looked up. "A pack of these cost an arm and a leg—as much as twenty-five cents!"

Alice and I stared at each other, the baffled look in her eyes mirroring my thoughts. Who in their right mind would pay that much money for cigarettes?

"Must have been someone who could afford such a luxury," I said thinking back to the funeral. I'd seen Matthew Britt smoking at the cemetery. Could this cigarette be his?

"The fog must have disoriented the driver."

Surprised, I spun toward the low, even voice and saw a tall, spare figure making his way toward me with a large fluffy collie by his side. He wore dark trousers held up by suspenders and a crisp white shirt, his lean face framed by thinning white hair. A pair of wire-rimmed spectacles perched on his nose. The brim of a dark fedora, tipped at an angle, shadowed his expression, giving him a quiet dignity as he approached.

"Drove straight into the tree," he continued. "Died instantly. Didn't know what hit her." He shook his head. "It's a shame."

His comments, so accurately spoken, caught me off guard. "Did you see the accident?"

"The fog was too thick," he replied with another shake of his head. "But I heard it. Laddie and I were a block away, taking our nightly walk when it happened. The car raced past us and seconds later it crashed. Are you investigative reporters?"

Panic shot through me. It didn't take him long to get suspicious. "Um…no," I replied quickly. "Eleanor and I were school friends. I'm Charlotte Johnson," I said using my maiden name, "and these are my cousins, Sean and Alice."

I grew up in Swede Hollow, the poorest neighborhood in St. Paul; an isolated ravine dotted with barebones shanties and outhouses built on stilts over Phalen creek. No one in Minneapolis—much less this ritzy neighborhood—had ever heard of me or my family, making it the perfect name to use.

The man smiled, revealing a gold tooth in the front of his mouth. "I'm Whit Crosby. I live just over the hill there." He pointed toward a large stone and brick mansion in the distance, its broad arches and asymmetrical towers rising above the treetops. "Laddie and I usually walk along the parkway every evening to get some exercise, but ever since the accident, we've been walking in the afternoon instead."

I looked back at the ruts in the ground. "I'm so sad about her death that my cousins agreed to drive me out here, hopefully to make some sense of why it happened."

Whit removed his hat and pressed it to his chest. "I'm so sorry for your loss, Miss. There was nothing I could do. She was already…gone…when I found her." He turned and walked toward the damaged tree. "She was slumped against the steering wheel. Must have hit her head on it." He looked toward the road, gesturing with his hand. "I flagged a passing car—a young couple on their way home—and asked them to call the police."

"Did you see anyone in the car with her as she passed by?"

"Well, that's the thing." Whit reached the tree and leaned against it using the flat of his hand. "My eyesight isn't the best at night. That and the fog made it impossible to see how many people were in the car, but I heard them arguing as it sped by so there must have been at least one passenger. When I got to the car, though, the woman was alone." He gazed at me, his expression troubled. "The police said it was probably noise from the wheels, but I know what I heard."

Of course you did, I thought, believing his story. *You probably heard Eleanor arguing with her fiancé. He could have left the scene after the crash and made it home on foot in fifteen minutes.*

But…why would Matthew leave her to die? Did he hate her that much?

"Do you recall hearing a man's voice?"

He frowned, the lines around his mouth deepening. "No, but I remember how different the voices were. That's why I knew she had a passenger."

I had hoped for more details than that but was grateful he'd taken the time to stop and talk.

"Laddie is getting restless," Whit said, gently patting the whining dog on the head. "It's been nice meeting you. I hope you find the answers you're looking for."

I thanked him and asked him if I could call him if I had any other questions. He graciously agreed and gave me his telephone number. Then I gestured to Sean and Alice that we should take our leave as well.

Regardless of what conclusions the police had drawn, I knew in my heart with absolute certainty, Eleanor hadn't died all alone.

Chapter Nine

"Change of plans," I said to Sean once we were back in the car. I glanced at my wristwatch. It was nearly two o'clock in the afternoon. The stop at the library had taken more time than I'd planned, and now it was way past lunch. "We're skipping the Britt residence today. Let's go home."

I needed to collect more information about Eleanor's relationship with her fiancé and her accident before I approached either of the Britts. I wanted to be fully armed with as many of the facts as I could gather so I knew if they were lying to me. Tomorrow, Sean and Alice would drive me to St. Cloud to speak with Dorothy Bloomer, the leader of Eleanor's book discussion group. Her name had been listed on the funeral program, so I knew who to track down.

Dorothy had spoken briefly at the funeral about Eleanor's dedication to the small group of women who met twice a month for lunch to discuss their latest book selection. She sounded as though she knew Eleanor quite well. That put her next on my list of people to interview.

On the way home, Sean stopped at a filling station for gas. I went into the station and purchased five-cent bottles of Coca Cola and bags of peanuts to tide us over until we got home. The bottles had been shoved into a barrel of melting ice to keep them chilled with a metal opener mounted on the wall to remove the caps. I was so parched, the cool sweet liquid slid down my throat, washing away the dust of the road and all my stress from the day.

When I arrived home, I shrugged out of my sweater and pulled off my hat, handing them off to Gerard with a smile before hurrying upstairs to the third-floor nursery. There, I found Will sitting in the rocking chair, holding Nora in his arms while Gretchen, my nanny, stood at the dressing table, busily changing Julien into his bedclothes.

"Hello, there, snuggle-bug," I cooed to Nora as I stepped into the room.

Ringlets of soft dark curls framed her face as she gazed up at Will with wide eyes, her cherub-like mouth alight with adoration, her tiny hand resting on his cheek. The golden lamplight cast a warm glow over them, gilding Nora's curls and relaxing Will's strong features.

He rocked her slowly, his smile gentle and unguarded as his large hands cradled her tiny body. The tough detective who carried the weight of other people's problems had vanished, replaced by the tender, loving father who held his child in his arms.

A deep calm settled over me as my heart aligned with his, knitting our little family together. Every time we stepped into this room, the tension of the outside world faded away, replaced by the love and happiness we experienced here.

Will glanced up from the rocker, smiling as our gazes met. "I've got some information for you," he said to me as I leaned over and kissed him on the cheek. "We'll talk about it after dinner."

"Okay," I replied, wondering what he'd learned. I was eager to find out but knew I'd have to wait. Will never talked about his cases in front of other people, especially our staff.

I measured a mere five feet, two inches tall, but Gretchen stood shorter than me. What she lacked in height, however, she made up for in efficiency and energy. She looked up long enough to give me a quick smile before fastening the last button on Julien's flannel nightgown. Then she lifted the boy from the wooden dressing table and handed him over to me.

"Hello, my adorable honeypot," I murmured softly as Julien smiled, revealing his tiny white teeth. "Mamma missed you today." His exuberant laugh sent a glistening stream of drool spilling down his chin and onto his blue bib. My heart swelled with love as I sat on the small sofa and held him on my lap, tickling him to make him laugh even more.

My sweet little man was growing so fast and looking more like Gus every day. Someday, he'd be tall and broad-shouldered like his father, with loose, sand-colored curls and sage-green eyes. Smart and resourceful. I wanted my son to succeed in whatever he pursued, but I vowed he would never end up in trouble with the Feds like Gus.

Will and I spent our nightly ritual with the children then kissed each one as Gretchen put them to bed. We walked together down the wide-open staircase and through the great hall to the dining room. Handcrafted sconces in the form of calla lilies embellished the wide doorway. By the time we reached the long, rectangular room with elaborately carved wainscoting and a crystal chandelier, it was exactly seven o'clock.

Francie decided to grace us with her presence tonight. She took her usual seat at the Chippendale table, across from me, her nose buried in the latest issue of Vogue magazine. She'd styled her natural blonde, chin-length hair with a side part and soft marcel waves, held in place with a black beaded headband. Pearl clusters graced her earlobes and for once, they weren't mine. Even though she had a huge closet filled with pretty clothes, she had a bad habit of helping herself to my wardrobe. Now that she worked part time at Madeline's cosmetics salon downstairs from my office, she had money to burn and spent every dime of it on her appearance—just like the other girls her age did.

I could have given her a weekly allowance, and I often did give her money for the cinema and other things, but I wanted her to understand the value of hard work and teach her how to manage her own finances responsibly. Francie, of course, always interpreted my restraint as a personal insult, convinced I was trying to clip her wings rather than teaching her how to use them.

Gerard seated me at the large Chippendale table set with china and crystal in his usual stoic fashion. He cleared his throat, as he often did when he wanted to draw my attention to something. Tonight, his gaze settled upon Francie with a disapproving stare, his lips pressed into a fine line, making it absolutely clear he did not approve of her dinner manners.

"Put away the magazine, Francie," I said gently, aware that my comment had the potential to ignite a firestorm. "It's inappropriate to read at the dinner table."

She flipped the magazine shut with a dramatic sigh, as if my request were the height of injustice. "Dinner in this place is so boring," she complained, rolling her eyes. "There's nobody to talk to. At least the magazine is *interesting*."

Will and I exchanged concerned looks, restraining ourselves from commenting.

What are we, chopped liver? his eyes seemed to say.

My husband rarely commented on my sister. He considered her to be within my domain and that included disciplining her. He had no desire to tangle with an emotional, high-strung sixteen-year-old—and no notion of how to handle her frequent tantrums—so he simply stayed out of it.

I don't know if it was the stress of the day, fatigue or both that made me lose composure, but when I caught the look on Will's face, it took every ounce of control not to burst out laughing. I hid behind my water glass, stifling the giggles that threatened to escape. Clowning around at dinner? Gerard would lay an egg!

We were well into the main course of baked ham with pineapple glaze when we heard a faint meow coming from the great hall. Francie stopped pouting about the magazine and glared at me with indignation.

I glared back. "What's wrong now?"

She let out a huff. "Why does Alice get to have a kitten, and I don't?"

Will stopped eating and grabbed his water glass. "Alice is a responsible person," he replied, surprising me with his remark. "She takes care of the kitten and doesn't shove the responsibility onto Cook."

Francie's soft lips formed a stubborn pout. "I *can* take care of a kitten! I just... haven't had the chance yet."

"We've been over this before," I added evenly. "You have a job, you have your friends, and you have school. When do you have time for a pet? It isn't a toy that you can keep in a box in your closet when you're not around. It needs love and attention. It needs you to *be home*."

"Well..." Francie said, her blinking eyes indicating that she was seriously weighing the sacrifices. Staying overnight with girlfriends, after school activities, her cinema nights, her work schedule at the salon... She paused, chewed thoughtfully, and then shrugged before returning to her dinner as if the problem had solved itself.

Was I this difficult at her age? Back then, I worked after school and on weekends, desperate to earn money to feed Mamma and Francie because my father was usually off somewhere on a drunken toot. Mamma's weak heart kept her bedridden and Francie was just a child, so it fell to me to take care of them. I guess I didn't have the luxury of deciding how much of my free time to give up for a pet. I didn't have any time to give away.

After dinner, Francie went into the drawing room to make her nightly telephone call to her best friend.

I followed Will into the library to discuss Eleanor's autopsy report. Bookcases and tall windows lined the walls. An oval table for studying and viewing maps filled the center of the room. Gerard had built a fire in the fireplace, filling the cozy room with crackling warmth. A bone china chocolate pot with a matching cup and saucer sat on the small oval table positioned between our wingback chairs. I shut the door behind me and made myself comfortable in my usual chair, feeling the warmth of the fire surrounding me like a blanket.

"Tell me about the autopsy report," I said as I poured myself a cup of hot cocoa from the tall, slender pot. "What did you find?"

From a hidden cupboard in the wall, Will produced a bottle of bootlegged whiskey and poured himself a small amount in a crystal glass. Slowly, he took a sip and sank into the chair next to me.

"She was thrust forward in the crash," Will said, his voice low, "hitting her forehead on the steering wheel and fracturing her skull. I'm sorry to say that she didn't die right away. According to the report, she would have been barely conscious but given the severity of the wound...I don't reckon she lasted long."

I gasped, wondering what her last moments had been like, hoping she hadn't suffered. "Dear God..."

Will didn't answer. He tossed back his whiskey and let the words hang in the air, giving me a moment to absorb the facts.

I sipped my rich, chocolatey drink as I pondered his words. "Did the report find any other health issues that might have caused the crash?"

"Bruises on her arms," he replied and glanced at the library door. "Possibly caused by an altercation of some kind. Other than that, she was in good health." He stood and placed a finger across his lips. Gently, he took the cup and saucer from my fingers, setting it back on the table. Then, taking my hands, he pulled me from the chair and led me into the den, shutting that door behind us as well. The den was only accessible from the library, which put two closed doors between us and anyone listening in the hallway. Surprised but curious, I folded my arms and stood patiently waiting for him to resume.

"There was one more item of considerable importance," he said, leaning against the ornately carved desk. It sat in the center of the small room, encased with tall windows and floor-to-ceiling bookcases containing an extensive collection of old, rare books collected by my late husband's father. "She was pregnant. By a couple of months."

I blinked, staring at Will in shock as my mind struggled to process this news. Eleanor Kimble pregnant? How sad to lose not one beautiful person, but two. Then again, if that was the case, who knew about it? Her mother? Matthew Kimble, surely...

Wait…if he was the passenger in the car when the accident happened, why would he leave her? It didn't make sense.

Now nothing made sense. I needed to go back to the beginning and think about this. Evaluate everything I'd learned so far. Something was wrong with my facts, but which ones?

"Gosh," I said, thinking furiously. "This changes everything."

"You need to proceed carefully now." He gently gripped my arms. "If this got out, it could destroy not only Eleanor's reputation, but the good name of the family as well. Not to mention yours."

I nodded dutifully. "I understand. I won't tell a soul, not even Ethel." I looked up. "But what about her mother? Shouldn't I talk to Marjorie about it?"

His dark brows furrowed. "It's a gamble. What if she doesn't know?"

I stared into his intense blue eyes. "Doesn't she have the *right* to know?"

He shrugged. "That depends. Some people can handle life-altering news. Others can't. If she's read the autopsy report or been told what it contained, she would already be informed. That is, if her daughter hadn't already broken the news to her."

"Absolutely," I replied. "But I'm not going to say anything about it yet to Marjorie. My next appointment with her is in a week, and I need to talk to a few people in the meantime to gather more facts."

Will nodded in agreement and opened the den door, standing aside for me to go first. "Good idea. Now, how are things going with Sean? Are you two getting along?"

I refrained from snorting my displeasure as I walked back into the library and sat down again. "He's pretty bossy, but I'm trying to work with him. I don't like the way he treats Alice, though. He finds fault with her constantly and often talks to her like she's beneath his contempt." I picked up the chocolate pot and refilled my cup with cocoa, my shaking hand attesting to my frustration. "Alice is disciplined, smart and trustworthy," I argued, setting the pot down. "She's a decent person and doesn't deserve to be disrespected by him or anyone else."

"I'll talk to him about it," Will said and picked up his drink again.

"I *have* been talking to him about it," I countered stubbornly, "and if he doesn't start listening to me, he's going to be dismissed."

"Let me handle it, Char. That's what you agreed to when we made this deal."

"I agreed to have protection," I shot back, my voice tightening, "not to be ordered around like I work for *him*."

He sighed, turning toward me. "You're not being ordered around. I just don't want you caught in the middle of something that could turn ugly."

I folded my hands around my cup, trying to still their tremor. "Then you'd better make sure Sean understands that too," I said quietly. "Because the next time he talks to Alice like that, I won't mince words with him."

Will's gaze met mine, steady and resigned. "Fair enough," he murmured. "But for heaven's sake, try not to start war under this roof."

I took a slow sip of cocoa; my gaze fixed on the fire. "That depends entirely on Sean," I said. "And whether he remembers who's in charge."

Chapter Ten

October 31st

The next morning, after breakfast, Sean, Alice, and I packed up and left for St. Cloud in the Ford to interview Dorothy Bloomer. The sunny, three-hour ride on Trunk Highway Ten started out paved, but soon the road turned to gravel, becoming bumpy as loose stones crunched under the tires, creating billows of dust in our wake. We passed miles of farm fields, now bare for the winter, stretches of open prairie, and scattered patches of oak, maple, and birch.

I attributed Sean's polite demeanor to Will's promise last night to speak with him about his attitude, but that didn't mean Sean was completely off the hook with me. I planned to closely monitor how he treated Alice when he thought I wasn't paying attention. As far as I was concerned, they were equals and each deserved to be treated with respect.

We pulled into a small roadside café on the outskirts of St. Cloud to eat lunch and check our map of the city. The aroma of simmering beef barley soup greeted us, stirring my hunger as we stepped through the door. Inside, wooden tables with mismatched chairs were tightly spaced on a gray marbled linoleum floor worn smooth by years of foot traffic. Farmers in bib overalls and working men of all ages filled the room. The air hummed with conversation and the clink of silverware on cream-colored stoneware plates. Only one square table in the back of the room remained unoccupied.

According to the telephone directory that our waitress had kindly supplied, Miss Bloomer lived a couple of blocks off St. Germain Street. We discussed our plans for the day over soup and sandwiches.

"I think we'll spend the night here," I said and pointed to the corner of St. Germain Street and Ninth Avenue on the map lying in the center of the table. "The Breen Hotel. Will has stayed there, and he highly recommends it."

I took a bite of my creamy chopped egg sandwich spread on hand-cut slices of homemade sourdough bread, thinking about our schedule. "I think we'll check in after we speak to Miss Bloomer. I'd like to get that out of the way first."

After lunch, we drove to Miss Bloomer's house, tucked in a small neighborhood within walking distance of downtown. She lived in a brown, wooden clapboard bungalow, its wide porch supported by tapered columns beneath a low-gabled roof. A lush green lawn surrounded the house, enclosed by a newly painted white picket fence. I stepped out of the car onto the grassy boulevard. The sharp scent of coal smoke lingered in the crisp autumn air. A slight breeze caused me to shiver and button up my double-breasted coat. The knee-length wool garment had a fur collar to keep my neck warm, but I still felt a chill as I opened the gate and walked up the sidewalk to the house.

Sean and Alice stayed behind in the car, watching me. Next door, a woman hung laundry from a clothesline that stretched from the back of her small garage to a T-shaped wooden post in the center of her lawn. She turned, casting a suspicious glance in my direction. I quickly stepped onto the porch, mindful not to crush the day's paper lying on the mat in front of the door.

I lifted the doorknocker and almost immediately the heavy door swung open. A young woman of medium height stood in the entrance wearing a loosely fitting cotton dress in teal with a drop waist, long sleeves, and a Peter Pan collar. Her short, light brown hair naturally streaked with blonde barely reached her jaw in a "helmet" bob. The short, blunt cut was all the rage nowadays, made popular by the silver screen actress, Louise Brooks.

Pungent aromas of fried bacon and fresh-brewed coffee wafted through the open doorway.

She glanced around to see if anyone had accompanied me. "May I help you?"

"Miss Bloomer?" I replied in the warmest, most caring tone I could muster. "Hello, I'm Charlotte Johnson, a friend of Eleanor Kimball's. I heard your testimony about her at the funeral. You sounded so warm and caring, I wondered if I might chat with you about her."

Dorothy's grayish-blue eyes shifted abruptly from curiosity to a cold, hard stare. "What about?"

Her sudden hostility caused me to pause.

They were supposed to be the best of friends, I thought, puzzled. *She had spoken so eloquently of Eleanor at the funeral. Why has her attitude suddenly changed? Did she really care about Eleanor, or was it just an act?*

"Eleanor and I went to high school together, but over the years, we lost track of each other," I said with a stitch in my voice to add to the illusion of grief. "I just wanted to learn more about her life since then." I placed my gloved hand over my heart and blinked to hold back non-existent tears. "I miss her so much."

"There's not much more to tell than what I said at the funeral," she replied with an indifferent shrug. "We met through the Minneapolis Women's Club, where Ellie's mother is a member. My cousin, Bea, works in hospitality there and met Ellie at a few club events where she volunteered. Bea invited her to visit our book discussion group, but we didn't expect a high-society girl like her to care about our lowly little bunch of small-town women. To our surprise, though, she showed up. After that first visit, she joined. We met twice a month."

"But she lived so far away," I said, curious to know why Eleanor would travel three hours each way just to talk about books. "Surely there were groups closer to home that she could have joined."

Dorothy folded her arms and glared at me. "Yes, but none of them were close to Henry Carpenter."

I blinked, thoroughly confused. "Who is Henry Carpenter and what does he have to do with Eleanor?"

Her eyes narrowed. "Why don't you ask him?"

"I will, but I need to know more about him."

"He's in the telephone directory," Dorothy snapped. "Look him up."

She proceeded to close the door in my face, but I stopped it with my foot. "Wait! Miss Bloomer, I'm sorry if I have offended you somehow. I just need to know a little more about this man, Henry Carpenter, and Eleanor's relationship to him."

Dorothy opened the door a few inches. "I have nothing more to say. My parents are due home any moment now, so I need to go." She stuck her head out the door and glanced toward the neighboring house. The lace curtain in the closest window fluttered slightly. "That old bat next door is spying on us." She pursed her lips, her nostrils flaring. "She'll be over here the minute you leave looking for gossip. Goodbye!"

Dorothy slammed the door in my face so hard, the newspaper on the mat bounced.

I turned away, wondering who Henry Carpenter was and what connection he had to Eleanor Kimball. And why his name had evoked such a strong response from Dorothy Bloomer. What information did she possess that she refused to divulge? Was he the father of her child? Was he the one who left her—and her baby—to suffer and die all alone to keep her secret buried forever?

Tomorrow's meeting with him promised to be interesting.

*   *   *

I walked slowly back to the car to arouse as little suspicion from "the old bat next door" as possible. Alice jumped out and held the door for me. I slid into the car and pulled off my gloves.

"Where to, Boss?" Sean asked, eyeing me in the rearview mirror, an item that I'd had specially installed in this car. "The hotel?"

"Yes," I said, tucking my gloves into my pockets. "I need to get us checked in and look up another name in the directory."

A few minutes later, we parked in front of the Breen Hotel, a red brick building with terra cotta detailing. I entered the lobby and took in the large, spacious room with plaster walls, oak wainscoting, ornate crown moldings, and hanging fixtures with frosted glass globes. On one wall hung pictures of beautiful birds. I studied the nightingale for a moment, fascinated by the delicate bird perched on a slender branch, its chest a warm, tawny brown, its wings subtly streaked with earthy tones. Something about the little bird intrigued me.

After a few moments, I approached the reception desk, a long, polished mahogany station in front of the elevators, and set my beaded purse on the counter. "I'd like three rooms, please."

Alice and Sean waited for me in the seating area, reclining on comfortable velvet chairs as I secured our lodging for the evening. According to the employee who checked me in, the hotel contained two restaurants, one that closed after lunch, and the other a high-priced bistro. There were also a barber shop and several exclusive boutiques. I wanted to spend time relaxing and browsing the shops but had to take care of business first.

Once we settled into our rooms, I returned to the lobby to place a call home using one of the hotel phones to let Will know I'd arrived. After I spoke to him, I browsed through the hotel's telephone directory for Henry Carpenter's address and telephone number. The operator on the switchboard placed the call for me. He answered on the fifth ring.

"Yes-s-s…" he said in a thick voice, slurring his words.

"Hello," I began in a businesslike voice. "Am I speaking to Mr. Henry Carpenter?"

"…yes-s-s." He paused. "Who's zis?"

I don't know why, but his question made me uneasy. "This is Charlotte Johnson. I'm a friend of Eleanor's. I—I'd like to speak with you about her."

An awkward silence fell over the line like a heavy curtain. "There's nothing to discuss," he said at last. "She's gone. Talking can't bring her back."

The deep, raw ache in his voice stirred something in my heart. "Sometimes it's healing for the soul to talk about your feelings," I replied softly.

"After what I did…nothing will heal my soul…"

His words sent a chill through me. "What did you do?"

I heard the faint clink of glass as he poured himself a drink. "I broke her heart…"

"You don't have to carry this burden alone," I said in a gentle but urging tone. "Please, let's meet. I really want to understand."

"Who did you say you were?"

"Charlotte Johnson."

"She never talked about you," he said, his tone laced with skepticism.

"We were good friends at school. Over the past few years, our lives have gone in different directions." I stared at the floor, desperate to steer the conversation away from me. "I'd like to meet later today. Perhaps over dinner—"

"Tomorrow," he said, bluntly interrupting me. "In the morning. My place."

"What time?"

"Early. Say, nine o'clock?"

"I'll be there," I replied, letting out a quiet sigh of relief. I'd make sure to arrive early—before he had the chance to ease his sorrow with whiskey. After thanking him, I hung up and stared at the receiver for a long moment. I didn't know who this man truly was or how he'd managed to break Eleanor's heart, but one thing was certain—tomorrow

I would find out.

* * *

After getting directions to Henry Carpenter's house from the bellhop on duty and a recommendation for a place to try local fare, I gave him a generous tip, and Alice, Sean and I went out for dinner. Down the street, we found the small, recommended café that promised home-cooked meals. Inside, wooden booths and small tables were filled with residents, their chatter blending with the clink of silverware. While we waited for our roast beef dinners, I leafed through the local paper, glancing at the headlines.

"This is a quiet town," I remarked, used to the bustle and bright lights of the city.

"You mean, boring," Sean scoffed. "Nothing but a bunch of farmers growing corn and making moonshine."

"I don't think that's correct," Alice stated in a bold tone. She reached inside her suit coat and pulled out a light tan playbill. "I found a stack of these in the lobby. There's a theater next to the hotel, and they're showing *The Black Pirate*." She smiled, showing her dimples, her brown eyes twinkling with excitement. "I've always wanted to go to the pictures and see Douglas Fairbanks."

Sean's scornful gaze cut her down before he even spoke. "We're here on business, see? This ain't no family vacation. We don't have time for that kind of nonsense!"

Alice sank low in her seat as guilt and humiliation shadowed her features, her shame unmistakable for speaking out of turn.

Sean's attempt to belittle her made me angry. "I think that's a wonderful idea," I said with a glare and a kick at Sean's ankle under the table. "It's been ages since I've been to the pictures. I haven't seen that movie, but Francie has, and she's been talking about it ever since."

Reaching across the table, I picked up the playbill and scanned it. "Showtime is at seven. We'll get there early to snag a good seat, okay? We'll grab a bag of fresh, hot popcorn and a soda and have a great evening watching the movie. Okay?"

Alice smiled with gratitude, but the pain in her eyes betrayed her. Sean's words cut deep, dampening her enthusiasm. Why did he have to take her to task like that for just being herself? Yes, she was different, but that was why I liked her. Why couldn't he accept her for who she was?

He was skating on very thin ice with me, and he knew it. One more incident like that and he'd be out on his ear looking for a new job.

Chapter Eleven

November 1st

The next morning, at nine o'clock sharp, Sean pulled the car up to the curb in front of Henry Carpenter's home. I stared through the window at the red brick, Queen Anne-style structure, wondering if he lived alone in this big house or with family. I certainly didn't want to find myself all alone with a strange man behind closed doors. Leaning forward, I tapped Alice on the shoulder.

"Yes, Miz Char?"

"Alice, you're coming in with me—as my sister—but we need to make a few changes to your appearance." I pulled off her black fedora and reached into my handbag for my lipstick. "Hold still," I said as I applied Max Factor Cherry Red to her lips. Then I pulled out my compact of rouge and lightly rubbed it along her cheekbones. I pulled back and gazed at her transformation. "There," I said with a smile. "The rouge makes your eye color stand out." I held out the compact that included a small mirror. "Take a look."

Alice stared into the mirror, transfixed by her reflection. "Jeepers, Miz Char. I never thought I'd look right with makeup, but I like it! I gotta get me one of these." She handed the compact back to me, her dimples deepening as she smiled.

Leaving Sean in the car, we walked up to the house together. I paused at the door, uncertain what I might find when someone answered it. I didn't have much time to wonder. The door flew open just as I rang the doorbell, echoing a loud *b-r-r-r-ing* in the chilly morning air. I froze, finding myself face-to-face with a tall, lean man in his forties. His black hair, graying at the temples, was in disarray, and his bloodshot eyes hinted at a long night with a bottle of hooch. A thick mustache lent him an air of distinction that didn't quite match the rumpled suit and crooked tie.

Clasping my hands together, I fought to keep from gasping. He was the same man I'd observed at the cemetery. The one who vanished after he caught me scrutinizing him.

I stepped forward, masking my shock behind a weak smile. "Mr. Carpenter?" If he recognized me as well, he didn't show it. At his nod, I stuck out my hand. "Hello, I'm Charlotte Johnson. Eleanor's friend. And this is my sister, Alice, who accompanied me here. Thank you for seeing me on such short notice."

Nodding again, he firmly shook my hand, then stepped aside to let us in. I walked into a wide foyer with cream walls, golden woodwork, and a high ceiling. The polished oak floor under my feet gleamed in the morning light. A magnificent, wood-paneled stairway curved upward toward the second floor.

"May I take your coats?" he inquired politely.

"Thank you."

He slipped the garment off my shoulders and hung it on a wooden coat tree in the corner, then assisted Alice. We followed him into the wide parlor, a bright, airy room with cream walls, tall windows, and a chandelier with etched glass shades. Light filtered softly through the floor-to-ceiling windows, casting an amber tone on the polished wood.

In the center of the room, a blue velvet settee and a pair of matching chairs faced each other on a circular Aubusson rug in cream wool, its intricate floral medallion woven in soft pinks, muted greens, and ivory. An oval, marble-topped coffee table sat in the center.

"Have a seat," he said courteously and gestured toward the settee. "Would you like coffee? My housekeeper makes it strong, just the way

I like it."

"Yes, that would be wonderful, thank you," I replied, impressed by not only his manners but the beauty of his majestic home.

"Yes, sir," Alice replied politely.

A silver coffee service rested on a tray on the coffee table next to a glass ashtray, a package of Turkish cigarettes, and a small silver pocket lighter with the initials HC engraved on it.

Ah, well, now I know whose cigarette butt fell out of Eleanor's car.

His hands shook as he leaned forward and began to pour a cup for me. "Cream or sugar?"

"No, thank you," I said, reaching for the steaming cup as the rich aroma of strong coffee filled my nostrils. "It smells so wonderful I'll just drink it the way it is.

He poured our coffee, adding a dollop of cream in Alice's brew, and grabbed the box of cigarettes. "Cigarette?"

"Thanks for the offer, but Alice and I don't smoke," I said and sipped my coffee, savoring the rich, full-bodied flavor as its warmth spread through me. "I haven't since before my son was born."

His hand froze in mid-air. "That happened to both of my sisters, too. Does the smell bother you now?"

"No." I shook my head. "Not at all."

A loud thump echoed above our heads. We all glanced upward.

"Pardon the noise. That's Juanita, my housekeeper," he said with an embarrassed grin.

I glanced across the parlor through a doorway to his office. His desk and a narrow table were piled high with papers. "That's a lot of paperwork you've got in there, Mr. Carpenter. You must be a busy man."

"Just call me Henry. I own a publishing house," he said as he lit a cigarette. "I do a lot of work at night in my office because during the day, it's too busy for me to get much reading done."

"Aren't you having coffee?" I asked, noticing that he hadn't poured himself a cup.

Nestling the cigarette in the crook between his first two fingers, he reached down next to his chair and picked up an open bottle of whiskey and a lowball glass. "Now that Ellie's gone, this is the only thing that gets me through the day."

"I'm so sorry for your loss," I said softly and pulled out my handkerchief, dabbing it at my nose to show sympathy. "You must have cared deeply for her."

He poured two fingers of amber liquid into the glass. "She was the love of my life." Shaking his head, he looked away, swallowing hard. "I don't know what I'm going to do without her." He tossed back the liquor and sat staring at the floor, his elbows resting on his knees as the smoke from the cigarette curled upward.

Since she was engaged to someone else, I didn't understand what he meant by that, but I didn't ask. Instead, I sipped my coffee and patiently waited for him to continue.

"You must have spoken to Dot," he said, frowning, and took a long drag off his cigarette. "Miss Bloomer. That's the only way you would have found out about me."

"Yes, I did, and she mentioned you, but she wouldn't tell me anything. She insinuated that you had something to do with her book discussion group."

Henry responded with a wry laugh and poured himself another shot of liquor. "I publish books and periodicals. I don't sit around and discuss them with a bunch of opinionated women." Lifting the glass, he took a swallow. "Dot and I have been friends for a couple of years. I've taken her out to dinner a few times, but it's nothing serious. One morning, I dropped her off at the library for her book discussion group, and Ellie was arriving at the same time, so Dot introduced us." He looked straight ahead, staring through the window. "I swear, it was love at first sight. For both of us."

"Ellie had a heart of gold," I said, manufacturing a sniffle to appear upset over losing a good friend. "I can understand why you'd be drawn to her."

He tossed back the rest of his drink and set the glass on the coffee table. "I hung around the library until their meeting ended, and as she was leaving, I approached her." He cleared his throat and looked up. "The first thing she said to me was how glad she was that I'd waited for her because she was curious about me, too. I asked her to have coffee with me, and by the time we parted that night, we knew we wanted to be together forever."

My mind spun with a thousand questions. At the time, did he have any idea what he was getting into?

I set my empty cup and saucer on the table. "Did you know then that she was engaged to Matthew Britt?"

"Of course," Henry said as he picked up the silver coffee pot and poured both Alice and me another cup. "There were no secrets between us." He set down the pot. "She was going to break the engagement, you know. She didn't love him—never did. The match was a financial arrangement between the parents. No one bothered to ask her what *she* wanted."

I picked up my cup and saucer again, needing something to hold while I dropped a bombshell on him. "They performed an autopsy on her. I…I know what was on the report."

He stared at me for a moment. "I saw the article in the paper about her accident and the funeral notice in the paper, but her father held back the information about her actual cause of death. How did she die? Did he kill her?" he asked, his face paling. "God knows they would have covered up the wound before her viewing at the funeral. Couldn't risk a scandal, you know."

"It was the accident. She was driving somewhere," I said, remembering how the bruise on Eleanor's forehead had been covered with heavy makeup. "It was dark, and the fog was so thick that she drove off the road into a tree, smashing her head into the steering wheel."

He set his bottle on the floor so hard, I started sloshing coffee onto my saucer.

"*He* did this to her," Henry shouted. "For revenge!"

"No one knows what actually happened, but there are questions," I said and set my coffee cup on the table before I dropped it. "I visited the crash scene and talked to an elderly man who walked that area with his dog every night. He swore that he heard two people arguing as the car sped by. By the time he reached the car, however, she was alone."

"Britt killed her," he said, his voice trembling with anger and heartbreak. "To punish her and get even with me."

I thought so too but refrained from saying so. "There was one more thing…"

He stared at me, long and hard, the anguish in his dark brown eyes revealing he already knew the secret I was about to disclose.

"I know she was with child," I said, "but her reputation is safe with Alice and me. We haven't spoken of it to a soul."

He sat back in his chair and released a deep, weary sigh of defeat. "We argued about it the day before her death…about breaking the news to her parents and then the Britts. I thought honesty was the only way. I wanted the world to know she was mine, that the child was ours. But Ellie… she was terrified. Old man Kimball is obsessed with his reputation. And Matthew Britt could ruin her reputation if he chose to get retribution on her and on her family as well. She begged me to keep it secret to protect her family from the truth until after we were married. I insisted that it was all going to come out anyway, thinking she'd see reason. I was convinced I was doing the right thing."

I shuddered to think of Robert Kimball's reaction. "I'm not so sure about that," I said doubtfully.

"We had a shouting match over it, and I… I was adamant, yes, but I wasn't cruel," Henry said as he covered his face with his hands. "After she left, I realized I'd been wrong. I had to apologize and promise her whatever she wanted. I wanted to give her peace, to let her fear ease, but I never got the chance. She was gone the next day. I never got to see her again. Never got to hold her and say I was sorry. That fight was the only one we ever had. It broke her heart, and I…" His tired eyes took on a haunted, faraway look. "I can't fix it. Not now. Not ever."

"One disagreement doesn't change a relationship," I said softly. "She knew she was loved. Don't trouble yourself over that."

The three of us sat in silence for a while as the clock on the mantel ticked steadily, filling the space between us.

"Maybe you're right," he murmured. "But I keep replaying that scene in my mind. Every word, every look. If I'd just—"

"You can't rewrite the past," I said, rising from the settee. Alice followed suit. "You can only decide what you'll do with it now."

It was time to take our leave. I'd put this poor man through enough for one day.

"After seeing the evidence so far, I agree with you, Henry. I believe she was murdered," I said plainly as I stood. "I don't know who was in that car with her, who abandoned her when she needed that person the most, but I'm going to find out. And when I do, Eleanor will get justice."

He set his drink on the table and stubbed out his cigarette. Rising from his chair, he accompanied us to the door and assisted us with our coats.

"I gave Ellie a diamond line bracelet for her birthday. She never went anywhere without it," Henry said gravely. "But on the day of her funeral, it wasn't on her wrist. I don't know if her mother removed it or if someone stole it from her at the scene. I realize I can't ask for it back, but if you could find out what happened to it, I'd be grateful."

"I'll ask her mother about it and let you know," I replied reassuringly as I buttoned up my coat. "If Mrs. Kimball doesn't know anything about it, I'll look elsewhere. Either way, I'll call you when I find out something."

He held the door for me. "Thank you. Mrs. Kimball would remember it if she saw it. It's an extraordinary piece with half-carat, emerald-cut diamonds in a platinum setting. I think you may want to talk to Dot again. She'd driven down to Minneapolis for an event given by the Historical Society and was supposed to have dinner with Ellie on the night she died. She would know if Ellie was wearing it."

His comment took me aback. "Oh, really? She failed to mention their dinner date when I spoke with her."

He gave me a skeptical look. "That doesn't surprise me. Dot has always been jealous of Ellie's relationship with me. Ellie planned to resign from the discussion group because of it, and she wanted to tell Dot in person. When Ellie drove Dot back to her hotel, maybe Dot decided to get even."

I suddenly remembered what he'd said earlier.

"I've taken her out to dinner a few times, but it's nothing serious."

I pondered that thought for a moment. Maybe not to him, but to Dorothy, a new door of opportunity had just opened. Eleanor's death paved the way for her to rekindle her relationship with him. Did she have anything to do with it?

I paused in the doorway, needing to get one more thing out in the open. "I'm sorry about staring at you at the funeral. I could see you were grieving, and it was rude. I didn't mean to draw attention to you and force you to leave."

He stared at me in puzzlement. "That's not why I left. Dot saw me and started weaving through the crowd to reach me. I had to escape."

"I'm glad you managed to dodge that bullet," I said as Alice and I walked out and stood on the open-air veranda. "Thank you for taking the time to speak with me."

He leaned one hand against the door, a grateful smile on his lean face. "Thank you for the information. Have a safe drive home."

I walked back to the car, determined to approach Dorothy Bloomer again and this time, get the truth.

* * *

"You haven't been honest with me," I said to Dorothy Bloomer as I stood on her front porch and glared at her. "You held back information—vital information that you knew I would want to hear. Why?"

Dorothy stood in the doorway, wrapped in a long burgundy sweater over a black dress, as defiant as ever. "Why should I tell you anything?"

"I can think of a few reasons," I said heatedly, "one being that you were the last person to see Ellie before she died." Leaning through the doorway, I confronted Dorothy nose to nose. "You were in the car with her when it crashed, weren't you? And when you saw she was dying, you abandoned her. Then you pinched her diamond bracelet as payment for her snatching your boyfriend out from under your nose!"

Dorothy's blue eyes widened as she angrily shoved me backward. "No, that's not true, you lying witch. I didn't kill her!"

We both glanced at the house next door, waiting for the curtain to move, but it remained motionless.

"Then what *did* happen?" I said coldly. "I'm listening, and this time, I want the truth."

She tightened the sash around her thick wool sweater and flipped up the collar. "We were supposed to meet for dinner, but Ellie never showed. I waited for an hour past the time she was supposed to pick me up at the hotel before I went out and had dinner *alone*."

"What time were you expecting her?"

Dorothy folded her arms tightly against the cold. "About seven o'clock."

Eleanor died approximately two hours after that. Plenty of time for dinner and a car crash—if she was lying.

"Can anyone attest to your story?"

Dorothy placed her hand on the door. "I don't know. The hotel wasn't busy that night. I went out the back door." She shivered. "I'm cold, and I don't like your tone. I don't feel like talking about this any longer."

"You're still in love with Henry, aren't you? You stayed friends with Ellie, but you've never forgiven her for stealing your beau, have you?"

She stepped back and slammed the door in my face.

I walked back to the car, bracing myself against the chilly breeze that had risen. Matthew Britt was still suspect number one—but after that door slammed in my face, Dorothy had just become suspect number two.

Chapter Twelve

November 2nd

"A benefit at the Britt's house?" With the receiver still to my ear and the candlestick telephone in my other hand, I collapsed onto the red damask settee in the drawing room of my home, shocked. "That's quite inappropriate if you ask me. Why, they're in mourning!"

"My dear, Betty's benefit for the Catholic orphanage is one of the premier events of the season," Ethel said on the other end of the line. "The sisters depend on her generosity to feed the children through the winter. She can't cancel it. Besides, as my guest, you'll have the perfect excuse to visit the Britts' home. It'll allow you to gather as many clues about their relationship with Eleanor as possible."

I wasn't sure how many clues I was going to gather at a fundraiser. After being gone for two days, I'd just arrived home from St. Cloud. I was tired and not in the mood to bathe, change, and go out again. I hadn't even had a chance to visit my children yet.

"I'm sorry to call you at the last minute," Ethel said, reading into my silence correctly. "I just received the invitation a few moments ago. It was delivered by one of the servants and was handwritten by Betty herself."

She paused long enough for me to wonder what else she wanted to say. Then I heard her draw in a deep, slow breath through her nose. "I must have been on a waiting list," she said suddenly, sounding miffed. "I wonder how many last-minute cancellations she had to fill before she got to *my* name. It would serve her right if I didn't go, but I'm doing this *for you*."

I stood in the drawing room with the receiver to my ear, so weak from fatigue that I was rendered speechless. I wanted to call it a day so badly, but there was no way I could get out of this. As it was, Ethel was upset about being relegated to Betty Britt's lowly alternate list. Making an excuse to skip it would not go over well. Regardless of how bitterly she complained, I knew Ethel was *dying* to go.

Charity benefits were *the* social events of the season among her crowd. They mixed glamour with philanthropy, and though they were for a good cause, they were just as much about being seen and showing off a person's status. The attendance list at the Britt's event would be a *who's who* of Minneapolis' elite. Everybody who was anybody would be there, and most of them were Ethel's friends.

Ethel, of course, was no slouch herself. The daughter of a Minnesota mining baron, she'd grown up in a world where debutante balls and dinner dances were as common as Sunday suppers for the rest of us. She carried herself with the kind of polished confidence that came from never having to question her place in society. The prospect of missing the Britt soirée wasn't merely disappointing—it was unthinkable.

"Is your husband going? I assume the invitation is addressed to you as a couple."

"Willard hates big, flashy social events," Ethel said briskly. "He'd rather spend his evenings playing cards and drinking brandy with his cronies at the Minneapolis Club."

The tension in her voice told me there was more to the story than she was letting on, but I let it go. Her marriage was none of my business, and I had no intention of prying into her personal life.

I rubbed my tired eyes with my free hand. "All right, but I'll meet you there. What time does it start?"

"Cocktail hour is at seven o'clock. The silent bidding starts at eight," Ethel replied with a happy ring in her voice. "One of my servants has exceptionally beautiful handwriting, and I'm having her make a couple of calling cards for you as Charlotte Johnson of Chicago, Illinois. This investigative business is becoming quite exciting!"

"I'll meet you there at eight," I said as an important thought crossed my mind. "Wait, just one more thing before I let you go. Do you know what happened to the diamond bracelet that Eleanor always wore? It wasn't on her wrist at the funeral. I recently found out that Henry Carpenter, the man I saw at the cemetery, gave it to her."

"Really…" Ethel replied. "I'll give Marjorie a call and ask her. You can fill in the rest of the details about that later tonight."

I hung up and went upstairs to see my children, then sank into a tub of hot water. The warmth eased the ache in my shoulders, but not the resistance lurking in the back of my mind. Ethel thrived on evenings like this—crystal chandeliers, champagne toasts, and whispered gossip behind feathered fans. I, on the other hand, would have traded it all for an evening with my husband in front of a calming fire, a pot of cocoa, and a quiet house.

Still, this was a great opportunity to see the Britts up close and possibly learn something new. I wasn't going for the champagne, the glitz, or the society chatter—I was going to learn anything I could about where the Britts were and what they were doing the night of Eleanor's death.

*   *   *

Errol, my chauffeur, pulled the limousine up to the Britt residence at exactly eight o'clock. I had relented tonight and agreed to use it to portray myself as a wealthy heiress from Chicago who came as Ethel's guest.

The last time I attended a gala like this one, someone recognized me as the former wife of a notorious bootlegger, and I was abruptly asked to leave. That was in St. Paul, where my late husband's reputation was well known. Hopefully, no one in the Minneapolis elite crowd would have any idea who I really was.

Sean and Alice accompanied me but agreed to stay behind with Errol so as not to arouse suspicion. They planned to mingle with the other chauffeurs idling along the curb, exchanging small talk and gossip in hopes of picking up something useful—any hint of what the Britts might be hiding, or what the servants knew about the days surrounding Eleanor's death.

Errol opened the car door and extended his hand to steady me as I slowly stepped out of the automobile, careful not to catch my heel on the edge of the running board. My gown, a beaded, sleeveless creation of ice-blue chiffon silk, fell in a graceful line to the sash around my hips, the straight skirt brushing the tops of my matching pumps. A fringed shawl draped my shoulders, elbow-length silk gloves covered my arms, and a beaded cloche hat framed my dark wavy hair. Diamonds glittering at my throat and ears, completing my outfit. Tonight's guests would be dressed to impress, putting their fortunes on display, and I intended to blend in seamlessly.

The Britt mansion was situated on Mount Curve Avenue, one of the city's most prestigious boulevards, where sprawling estates lined the road in a showcase of opulence. Grand façades of limestone and brick, sweeping porticos, and manicured lawns edged with wrought-iron fencing set them apart from the rest of the city.

The large, multi-story brick mansion had high, rectangular chimneys jutting from both sides of the roof and a central dormer in the front. Warm golden light spilled from the tall, multi-paned windows, beckoning me as I strolled along the sidewalk in the unusually balmy November air to a set of stone steps that led to a wide front porch under a graceful portico supported by Corinthian columns.

Overhead, a bright harvest moon glowed deep orange among the stars against a clear indigo sky. I drew in a deep, calming breath, wishing I could forego the festivities and lose myself instead in a quiet walk through this elegant neighborhood.

Ethel stood inside the entrance of twin leaded glass doors in a long gold dress, chatting with a tall, gray-haired man in a black tuxedo.

Large ruby pendants adorned her neck and ears. Her thick gray hair had been swept to the crown of her head and held in place with ruby and diamond combs.

The moment our gazes met, she excused herself and swiftly walked toward me. "My dear, you look wonderful," she said, hugging me. "Come along. It's chilly out here, and we have important work to do."

Unease seeped into my thoughts. Ethel's growing interest in becoming my sidekick began to worry me. Did she really think we were in this together? I had nothing but the deepest gratitude for her continued support, but I would never forgive myself if anything happened to her while investigating a case with me.

Two liveried servants stood at the double entrance doors, welcoming us. Once inside, another servant took my shawl. Ethel handed two calling cards to the butler, who checked our names against his list. A moment later, his deep voice carried through the grand foyer: "Mrs. Willard Rogers of Minneapolis, with Miss Charlotte Johnson of Chicago."

My stomach fluttered. Would anyone recognize me? Would I be called out publicly like the ladies of the St. Paul Friendship Club had purposely done to humiliate me?

Ethel and I stepped into a large drawing room filled with a sea of glittering gowns and tailored tuxedos. The soft glow of crystal chandeliers bounced off gilded mirrors and oil portraits lining the walls. The air was fragrant with fresh-cut roses and the pungent aroma of cigarette smoke. Gentle music from a string quartet floated above the hum of conversation, punctuated by an occasional burst of laughter. Men gathered in small groups talking politics, business, or the stock market. The women clustered around the fireplace and the buffet, sipping champagne from crystal flutes, eating delicacies, and sharing gossip. No one seemed to care that we were in the throes of Prohibition or that many people were struggling just to make ends meet. These people lived in a glittering bubble of wealth, untouched by the everyday issues that defined the lives of ordinary people.

Strangely, I didn't see one picture of Eleanor and Matthew together anywhere. It was as if she'd never been in his life.

A female servant in a black dress and starched white apron approached us, holding a small round tray containing crystal flutes. "Champagne for you? Or perhaps ginger ale?"

Ethel selected a flute of champagne. I opted for ginger ale; grateful I could pass for one of them without having to swill the stuff.

"This party must have cost the Britts a small fortune," Ethel murmured to me in between sips of champagne. "Given their financial situation, one wonders who they had to blackmail to get enough cash to pull it off…"

I was so tired, I almost burst out laughing. Ethel saved me the embarrassment of making a spectacle of myself by walking straight toward Betty Britt.

"Oh, there you are," Ethel said to the short, stocky woman in a long-sleeved, floor-length gown of rich emerald silk. Betty wore round spectacles with Black Hills gold frames etched with delicate leaf motifs. Her softly waved salt-and-pepper hair was gathered into a sleek chignon at the nape of her neck. The emeralds and diamonds clustered at her throat glistened in the soft light. "It's great to see you, Betty. I love your new glasses. They're beautiful!" She went to hug the woman, but Betty pulled away, wincing at Ethel's hand on her left shoulder. "What's the matter? Are you alright?"

"My bursitis is flaring up again," Betty replied in a tight voice, her brows creasing from the pain. "It's been bothering me ever since—" She shook her head in annoyance. "Never mind. It hurts like the devil tonight, but it's nothing serious."

"You must have pushed yourself too hard with all these benefit preparations," Ethel scolded. "You need to slow down before that shoulder gives out entirely."

Betty shook her head. "A little pain never stopped me before.

Once this benefit is over, I'll take a few days to rest." She turned to me, studying my face. "You look familiar. Have we met?"

"I'd like you to meet Charlotte Johnson," Ethel cut in before I could reply. "She's visiting from Chicago."

Betty's eyes widened with recognition. "Wait…I remember you now. I saw you at the funeral. You made such a scene you had to be escorted out by Pastor Olafson."

My cheeks grew hot with embarrassment. How many other people here had noticed that I'd made a colossal fool of myself? "I-I didn't mean to get so upset," I replied, stumbling over my words. "But I was so saddened by Eleanor's death, I couldn't help myself."

Betty's blue eyes narrowed behind her exquisite glasses. "You and she were friends? She never mentioned you."

"We were inseparable in school, but after we graduated, we lost track of each other," I said, trying to sound convincing. "Not long ago, we ran into each other at the Tea Room in Dayton's Department store. We set a date to meet for lunch. There was something she wanted to talk to me about, but she never got the chance to tell me what it was. She died the next day." I studied her closely, searching for any hint of the friction between her and Eleanor. "Do you have any idea what that might be?"

Betty froze for a moment, her silent stare unflinching. Then she glanced away, impatient to finish her conversation and move on. "Not at all. How long will you be staying in town?"

"A few more days," I replied innocently.

"We must visit again before you leave." She patted my hand to appear caring, but it was obvious she'd already lost interest in me as she stared at someone past my shoulder.

I stepped aside and sipped my ginger ale, happy to escape her scrutiny.

"Well, that got the old girl in a flap," Ethel whispered to me after Betty left us. "Let's see how long it takes before she spills the beans about your conversation with Eleanor to her son." She leaned closer. "Be careful around that one. He's quite the ladies' man. I hear he's got a string of notches on his belt to prove it."

"Don't worry about me," I said as I watched Betty greet a couple who had just been announced. "I can handle myself."

"I spoke to Marjorie today," Ethel murmured. "She's appalled at the Britts for not postponing this event. Says she'll never speak to Betty again for disrespecting Eleanor's memory." She leaned even closer. "And by the way…she doesn't know what happened to the bracelet. According to Robert, Eleanor wasn't wearing it when her body arrived at the morgue."

I mulled over that as we sipped our cocktails and wandered into the sunroom where the auction items were displayed. At the door, a servant manned a wood donation box for attendees. I filled out an envelope, stuffed it with cash, then slipped it through the slot at the top.

Along the back of the window-lined room, small tables gleamed beneath shaded lamps, each draped in ivory lace and bearing an item. I strolled along slowly, examining a pearl necklace, a silk scarf, sculptures, imported chocolates, gourmet baskets, a weekend at a Duluth estate, and other treasures. Beside every display sat a crystal bowl filled with folded bid cards, a discreet alternative to the noisy auctions of lesser events. All around me, couples lingered to admire the items, writing their bids on the cards and placing them in the bowl beside each item. A servant would later collect them for review.

I placed a bid on a painting of the lighthouse on Lake Superior and paused to admire it.

"That's a wise choice," a smooth, masculine voice echoed over my shoulder. "The artist is slowly gaining recognition for his work, and the painting is sure to gain value in the future."

I spun around and found myself staring into the piercing blue eyes of Matthew Britt. My number one suspect.

Chapter Thirteen

In the sunroom at the Britt charity benefit, Matthew Britt's mass of curly blond hair created a striking contrast to the crisp black of his tailored tuxedo. He stood so close, his breath brushed my skin as his blue-eyed gaze burned into mine, making no secret of his attraction to me. His easy, beguiling smile displayed the bold confidence of a man accustomed to always getting his way.

"You've got excellent taste in art," he said, his voice carrying a sensual lilt as he pointed toward the lighthouse painting. "Something I find very appealing in a woman."

If his bold flirtation was intended to sweep me off my feet, it failed. I found his cockiness instantly repulsive.

"Oh, really?" I said sharply as I stared at the thin reddish mustache tracing his upper lip. "Are you an expert in such things, or is your opinion simply to get me to bid higher?"

His gaze roamed over me like a challenge, smooth and unhurried. "Whatever you say, sweetheart."

Nine years of marriage to a wealthy bootlegger and a powerful businessman in the underworld had taught me many things, including how to handle myself around a slick Casanova like Matthew Britt. Besides insulting, it was hardly the behavior of a man mourning the death of his fiancée. I kept my expression cool, my voice dripping with disdain.

Let the game begin…

"I'm not your sweetheart."

"You could be if you wanted to," he replied smoothly. "A woman like you would be a great asset to a man like me. In return, I could make you very, very happy."

A great asset? Me—or my money? I almost burst out laughing at the absurdity of his assumption that I wanted—or needed—anything he had to offer.

Placing my hand on his chest, I pushed him away. "Have you no shame? I know who you are, Mr. Britt. Your fiancée has recently passed away. Show her some respect!"

"And I know who you are," he stated, dropping all pretense of friendliness. "*Miss Johnson.*"

I held his gaze, unflinching. Betty must have already informed him that an eligible young pigeon…ahem…heiress from Chicago had arrived. "Word travels fast in this house."

"That depends on who we're talking about."

Gripping my beaded clutch, I still managed to fold my arms into a tight bow to keep his gaze from dropping to my breasts. The hungry look in his eyes gave me the chills and repulsed me at the same time. Did he suspect I wasn't who I claimed to be? I needed a diversion to steer his interest away from me. "Then let's talk about *her*. Did you have anything to do with Ellie's death?"

His laugh sounded hollow as he furtively glanced around to make sure no one was eavesdropping. "Don't be absurd. Why would I kill my future wife?"

I stared hard into his eyes, not in the mood for his innocent act. "I don't know. You tell me. I know she didn't love you."

His smile faded at my accusation. "The marriage was arranged by our parents for their mutual benefit, but in time, Ellie and I would have grown to love each other."

"Unless she came to her senses and changed her mind."

He went very still, his eyes turning hard as stone. "Is that what she told you?"

"She didn't have to," I said, sidestepping the question. "The bruises on her arms told a story of their own."

The room fell into an uneasy silence as our contentious sparring caused people to stare at us. Clenching his fingers around my arm, he escorted me from the room, pulling me into an empty hallway.

"Take your hands off me!" I snapped, wrenching my arm from his vise-like grip.

He towered over me as a menacing frown darkened his face. "What are you getting at? That I killed her out of pride because she was going to show me the door? Listen, doll, keep your mouth shut if you know what's good for you. Spreading rumors about things you know nothing about could land you in a nasty jam."

Vigorously rubbing the red marks his grip had made on my arm, I looked up, confronting his angry glare. "Is that a threat? If it is, I'm not afraid of you, and I'm not going to stop asking questions because I believe the old man's story—the one who saw her car just before it crashed. He swore that someone else was with Ellie that night, arguing with her. I think the person forced her to drive off the road and collide with a tree, then abandoned her to die all alone. You," I said, poking my finger in his chest, "you're the only person who has a motive! I intend to find out who was in that car with her, and I'm not going to stop until I do."

Matthew's face flushed, his eyes blinking furiously. He shoved my hand away. "She's gone, and none of your meddling will bring her back. Leave it alone, or I guarantee you'll be sorry!"

But I wasn't ready to leave it alone. I still had one more burning question to lob at him. "What did you do with her diamond bracelet?"

His brows furrowed, his eyes narrowing with anger. "What bracelet? I don't know what you're talking about."

"Don't insult me with your lies," I snapped. "You know very well what bracelet I'm talking about. She wore it all the time."

"She had a lot of jewelry," he replied with a careless shrug. "The pieces from Ellie's grandmother were the valuable ones, but her mother never let those rocks out of her sight. Why would I care about some silly bracelet?" He snorted. "I want my engagement ring back. It belonged to *my* grandmother!"

"This was no ordinary trinket," I shot back. "Each of the stones weighed a half-carat. It was worth a small fortune. A tempting piece for someone who's on the verge of bankruptcy!"

"Who do you think you are, you little—" Lunging forward, he reached for my hair, a major miscalculation on his part. Had he succeeded in knocking my hat off just to grab a hunk of my locks, he would have been walking like a crippled jackass for the rest of the evening. Bracing my free hand on the wall, I snapped my head out of reach and shifted my weight, prepared to make a swift kick with my knee when—

"Charlotte, dear, I've been searching everywhere for you! Come with me," Ethel said breathlessly as she burst into the hallway, interrupting us. She grabbed my arm and pulled me away from Matthew just in time to spare one of us from disaster.

"I had to interfere," she said as she led me back to the drawing room. "Your voices were so loud that heads were turning."

"What a shame. We were just getting started," I replied, rolling my eyes as she steered me through the elbow-to-elbow throng of people, chatting and drinking champagne. The smoky air, blue with cigarette haze stung my eyes, but it didn't stop my mind from angrily replaying the scene with that infuriating man. Matthew Britt was not the gentleman he pretended to be. He had a breaking point, and I'd just pushed him past it. I had no doubt he was lying straight to my face. Why else would he have become so ugly? "Where are we going?"

"To get a bit of fresh air," Ethel said as we approached the servant manning the coat closet. "I think *someone* needs to cool down."

We retrieved our wraps and left the house, taking in the unseasonably warm air of the evening. The sky had clouded over, concealing the moon and making the night darker than ever.

I drew in a deep breath as we strolled toward the boulevard. "As long as we're taking a breather, let's walk for a while. I'd love to see more of this neighborhood."

I didn't see Errol anywhere and assumed he'd stayed with the limousine. Sean and Alice leaned against the fender of a Cadillac parked at the curb, chatting with a couple of chauffeurs, but they sprang to attention when they saw us coming toward them.

"Leaving already?" Sean asked, the surprise in his voice indicating that he hadn't expected me to leave the party so soon.

"Not at all." I waved the notion away as we approached them. "We're just getting some fresh air. It's very smoky in the house."

Automobiles sat bumper-to-bumper on both sides of the paved street, but there was no live traffic to speak of during this time of night. Ethel and I stepped out into the roadway and leisurely walked, taking in the scenery along our way. Sean and Alice fell into step behind us.

"Well," I said over my shoulder to them, "did you learn anything new tonight?"

"Yes, Miz Char—" Alice started to say before Sean cut her off.

"Some of the people invited turned down the offer," he said quickly. "They were upset that the Britts were throwing a party so soon after Miss Eleanor Kimball's death. It was disrespectful."

"Hmph. So that's why I was invited at the last minute," Ethel murmured.

"Mr. Britt argued with Miz Eleanor the night she died," Alice said timidly.

I spun around and stared at her, stunned at this new revelation.

"Where'd you hear that?" Sean bellowed with a jealous edge in his voice. "Don't be making claims unless you know they're true!"

Alice's face paled at having her integrity questioned. She shrank back, lowering her gaze. "I went around to the back of the house to use the servants' privy, and I heard the staff talkin' about it." She hung her head. "I—I don't know if it's true. I'm sorry, Miz Char."

"No need to apologize for that," I said, placing my hand on her shoulder while at the same time giving Sean a disapproving glare. "It's my job to find out whether it's true or not. You did exactly what I asked you to do."

We walked in silence for a while, taking in the scenery as I mulled over Alice's news. If Mathew and Eleanor fought that night, what was it about? What time did it happen? Did they leave together? I wish I had a way to talk to Betty's servants without her finding out, but after my shouting match with Matthew, I was probably the subject of their gossip now.

In the distance, the roar of an automobile speeding down the street prompted us to move to one side, standing next to the boulevard. As the headlights came closer, I expected the car to slow down, but instead, it sped up, and it appeared to be weaving all over the road.

"Watch out!" Sean shouted as the car veered toward us, its headlights blinding us. He grabbed my shoulders and pulled me out of the way. Alice acted quickly, pulling Ethel to safety just as the black car careened in our direction, driving over the curb and nearly striking us.

"Someone had too much champagne at the benefit," Ethel said, sounding dazed as we watched it speed away.

"I don't know. That looked intentional," Sean said gravely. "That Model T was going at top speed. It swerved right into our path."

Top speed for a Model T was forty to forty-five miles an hour. I knew that because I owned a Ford and used to drive it every day. Breathing hard from shock, I blinked, still adjusting my eyes. "Did you see who it was?"

I had no idea how many people heard Matthew and me arguing, but if it was intentional, obviously someone didn't want me to bother him ever again. Did someone at the party come after me, or was it Matthew? I inhaled a deep breath. He couldn't be that stupid, could he?

"No, it was too dark to see inside the car. The headlights were too bright." Sean shook his head and stared down the road at the disappearing automobile. "This was no accident. I think it's time to pull the plug on this investigation. The situation is getting too dangerous."

I blinked, stunned at his boldness. "What do you mean?"

"Look," Sean said forcefully, raising his voice. "I gave Will my word that I'd keep you safe, and I intend to do that. When he finds out what happened tonight, he'll back me up. It's over. We're going home."

This was the last straw. Sean McBride just admitted that he had worked for Will all along—not me. No wonder he'd been so belligerent whenever we disagreed. He'd been working against me, not for me. And now he believed he had the power to shut the investigation down. But not anymore.

"I'm not going anywhere with you," I said with finality. "You don't give me orders. You're fired."

Ethel did a double take. Alice gasped.

"You can't fire me," he said with an arrogant grin. "You didn't hire me."

"Then go to work for my husband," I countered, raising my voice to match his. "Because you're done working with me. I said, go!"

"Fine, but you're making a big mistake, lady." Sean backed away and walked swiftly down the street. I hoped I never saw him again.

"Maybe being an investigator isn't so exciting after all," Ethel murmured. She sounded shaken, upset.

"Ethel, I don't feel like going back to the benefit," I said slowly, already preoccupied with what I would say to Will. He was not going to be happy—but he knew how unhappy I'd been with Sean McBride. "Do you mind if we call it a night?"

She gazed at me with tired eyes. "Not at all. I could use a hot bath and a hot toddy myself."

I turned to Alice. "Find Errol and tell him to pick me up in front of the Britt house."

Back at the Britt mansion, I said goodbye to Betty Britt and thanked her for a wonderful evening. Ethel and I were saying our goodbyes as Errol and Alice pulled up in the car.

We were all silent on the ride home. The car pulled into the carriage porch, and Alice jumped out. Not waiting for Errol, she jerked open my door and assisted me out of the car.

"Don't worry, Miz Char," she said to me as I alighted from the back seat. "Until we find someone to replace Sean, I'll do everything in my power to protect you. I won't let you down."

Her sincerity touched me so deeply that I struggled to keep my emotions under control. "I know you will, Alice," I said in a trembling voice as I patted her shoulder. "That's why I hired you. You're a good kid."

As I walked up the steps, the door opened, and my husband stood in the entrance, a deep frown etched on the lean planes of his face. Obviously, Sean had talked the Britt staff into letting him use the telephone to call Will and tattle on me, giving the Britt staff even more reason to gossip about me.

"We need to talk about what happened tonight," he said in a deep voice. "*Now.*"

"Will, it's not what you think," I argued defensively. "I didn't fire him just because I didn't like him."

He stood aside for me to enter. "We'll discuss that later. I'm talking about *you*. It doesn't matter why you and he parted ways. You know what you agreed to before I hired him, Char. No bodyguards, no investigative office."

It irritated me that he would take such a hard line with me, but I knew it wouldn't do any good to put up a fuss about it because I didn't have a leg to stand on. I understood fully what I'd agreed to, and everything would have worked out if Will had let me hire my own help in the first place. This time I would do it *my* way.

I just needed to convince him of that…

Chapter Fourteen

"Sean McBride is impossible to deal with," I said to Will as we stood in the library with the door closed. Burning logs crackled in the fireplace, filling the room with toasty warmth. Tiffany lamps with dragonfly-themed shades cast a warm, jeweled glow across the room. "He challenges every decision I make, as though he thinks he somehow has jurisdiction over me. I pay his salary, not the other way around. I refuse to allow him to order me around like that."

"I hoped you two could settle your differences and learn to work together," Will said sounding disappointed as he poured himself a shot of his favorite whiskey. He didn't drink often, but lately, he'd been having a drink every night. Was I causing him so much consternation that he had to drink to calm his nerves? "Sean came highly recommended."

"He was highly disagreeable if you ask me," I replied, getting upset that Will wasn't seeing the issue from my perspective. "I tolerated his criticism of using the Ford, and I had to continually correct his disrespectful behavior towards Alice, but when he tried to undermine my authority by announcing—in front of Ethel, mind you—he was shutting down *my* investigation, that was the last straw. I sent him packing."

"According to Sean, someone tried to run you down," Will said, changing the subject. Cupping his hand under my chin, he gave me a worried look. "This is why I insist you have protection, Char. What would you have done if he wasn't there?"

Got out of the way... I thought sarcastically to myself. *I don't need a man to save me every time something happens!*

"Will," I argued, "we were at a party where the champagne was flowing like water. What did you expect? Someone got sozzled and decided it was time to go home. They probably didn't expect to see a bunch of people walking along the road at that time of night."

The glass in his hand stilled mid-air. "What exactly were you doing walking around outdoors after dark?"

Exhaustion suddenly washed over me. The evening had taken a deeper toll than I'd realized. Facing the fire, I leaned my arm on the back of my easy chair and sighed. "It wasn't even my idea. I'd just had a spirited discussion with Matthew Britt and Ethel suggested we go for a walk to get some air. My eyes were burning from all the smoke in the house, so I agreed. No one knew we were leaving. It was just a coincidence."

Will shook his head. "I don't believe in coincidences when it comes to murder, and neither should you. Never assume that the simplest explanation is the right one when you're investigating a case, understand? Look deeper, Char. There's always a thread, and someone is counting on you to miss it."

"All right," I replied, though the more I replayed the incident in my mind, the more I doubted his logic applied to this case. No one knew we were leaving the house.

Will set his glass on the table and slid his hands around my waist, pulling me close. The warm drift of whiskey on his breath brushed my cheek. "You're not going to agree with me on this, but I don't care. Until we hire a new bodyguard, your investigation is on hold."

"What?" I stared up at him, my palms resting on his shoulders. "Why? I still have Alice. She's as smart and tough as any man. Besides, I can't just stop working on this case. The trail will go cold!"

His stern expression didn't waver. "I won't allow you to

investigate a possible murder without adequate protection. Is that understood?"

"But Will," I protested, my voice rising, "I'm meeting with Marjorie Kimball on Saturday, and I promised her I'd have some answers. I can't let her down!"

"I meant what I said, Char. Everything is on hold until Sean is replaced."

Weariness pressed down on me like a heavy cloak. I could barely think, let alone keep arguing. A night's rest was the only thing that would untangle my thoughts. I exhaled a long sigh as tears of frustration pricked my eyes. I'd given Majorie my word; I couldn't fail her.

"Then I guess I'd better start looking for a new bodyguard first thing tomorrow."

* * *

November 3rd

The next morning, Alice and I went to my office to catch up on paperwork. I needed to put my notes in order and study what information I had gathered so far. After that, I planned to visit a friend and ask him for some much-needed advice.

"I'll drive to the office," I said to Alice as we walked together down the driveway to the large garage behind the house to get the Ford. Normally, Gerard would send someone to inform Errol that I wanted the car to be brought around to the carriage porch, but I felt like taking a brisk walk in the crisp, sunny morning air.

Alice's face crumpled with hurt as she tipped her fedora back on her head with her thumb. "Don't you trust me?"

"Of course, I do," I replied quickly. "It's just that I rarely get to drive nowadays and I really enjoy it. Besides, I'm worried that if I don't get a little practice occasionally, I'll forget how." I smiled reassuringly. "I'm excited. This will be my first time behind the wheel of the new Ford. You can drive home, okay?"

"Yes, ma'am," Alice replied with a grin.

If I had any doubts about my ability to drive after not getting behind the wheel for several months, they vanished the moment I drove through the gates of my property, waved at Chet, my daytime security guard, and turned into the flow of traffic on Summit Avenue. It was as if I'd driven only yesterday. My hands and feet automatically performed their duties without so much as a second thought.

*   *   *

At the office, I spent an hour organizing my notes, recording on a writing tablet everything that I'd learned so far. I already had a significant amount of information to share with Marjorie, but I wanted to be able to say with certainty that I had a solid lead on who was in the car with Eleanor. So far, I only had my suspicions.

When I finished my paperwork, I put it in my desk drawer and went down to the car. Sliding onto the seat of the passenger side I turned to Alice. "Your turn to drive. Take me downtown St. Paul."

"That place is confusing," Alice said as she put the car into gear and began to drive down the alley behind my office building. "All the streets downtown curve this way and that. Take a wrong turn and you could find yourself halfway to Minneapolis before you figure out what went wrong."

We laughed.

"We're going to the Endicott Building on Fourth Street," I said. "I've been there before, so I'll direct you where to go."

Alice turned onto Summit Avenue and quickly gained speed to keep up with the flow of traffic. "Who are we going to see?" She gave me a worried look. She knew Will had forbidden me to investigate the case until we'd obtained a replacement for Sean.

"We're not working on the case," I assured her. "Well, not exactly. I'm going to visit Leon Goldman to hopefully get a few leads on a new bodyguard."

Alice did a double take. "But Miz Char, he's a dangerous criminal!"

"As unlikely as it sounds, he's been good to me," I said, turning in my seat to face her. "Leon and my late husband, Gus, were mortal enemies, so I never met him while Gus was alive. But last year, when Leon's nephew started sniffing around Francie, I stormed over to his office to put a stop to it."

A laugh bubbled up in my chest. It was funny now, but not back then. "I was so furious about that young man getting tangled up with my sister, I didn't care how dangerous Leon was—not when Francie's future was on the line. I barged into his office and told him flat-out that he could warn his nephew off, or *I would*."

Alice glanced at me, shocked. "You really told him that?"

"Yes, I did," I said chuckling. "He thought my threat was the funniest thing he'd ever heard. And that made me even angrier. But he did what I asked, and we've been friends ever since." I shook my head. "Oh, we're not close. He knows Will and they've spoken on numerous occasions but I'm not part of that crowd any longer." I folded my arms and stared at the stately homes along Summit Avenue as we rode along. "When Gus died, I left that world behind and I'll never go back."

Alice sent me a sideways glance. "Do you think he'll help you?"

"I don't know," I said apprehensively. "But it's worth a try."

Once we arrived downtown, I directed Alice to park behind a long, narrow structure housing a bank next to the Endicott Building. We parked and crossed the alley between the buildings. We entered the rear lobby of the Endicott Building and waited for the elevator car to arrive.

"Tenth floor please," I said to the elevator operator when we stepped inside. The white-haired woman in a gray uniform extended her white gloved hand, pulling the glass door and metal scissor gate closed. Then she pushed the lever down on the manual control and the elevator slowly glided upward. As soon as she stopped the car at our floor and opened the door, I stepped out and headed to the end of a long hallway to a door that had no name painted on the yellowed pebble glass.

I pushed open the door and found Leon Goldman's secretary, Maisie—a woman about my age with cropped auburn hair and wearing a sage-colored flapper dress. She stood by the window, looking bored as she gazed down at the street, but the moment she saw me, her posture changed. Her eyes flared like a wildcat about to strike.

"Oh," she sneered when she recognized me. "It's *you*."

Alice entered the room behind me and shut the door, nervously glancing around as her hand slipped inside her coat, ready to pull her gun if danger arose.

I smiled, ignoring the way Maisie's jealousy reared its ugly head whenever another woman got within spitting distance of her boss—her *married* boss. "I need to speak with Leon."

Maisie walked toward her desk, her gaze sweeping over me with barely concealed disdain. "You don't have an appointment," she said in a slightly nasal, overly feminine voice, "and he's busy."

"I don't need one," I countered and reciprocated with a dismissive look as I walked to the closed door of Leon's office and knocked. "Leon," I said loudly, "it's Char. I need to talk to you. It's important."

I knew better than to just burst in unannounced. I did that once and found myself staring down the barrels of a pair of loaded pistols. Leon's bodyguards didn't take kindly to surprises.

The door suddenly swung open and Blackie filled the doorway—a tall, kohl-haired brute with a permanent five-o'clock shadow, wide shoulders, and a dark suit stretched tight across his muscular frame. He greeted me with a broad grin, but his gaze automatically swept over me in a quick, practiced search for a weapon.

"Good morning, Miss Char." His eyes narrowed as his gaze shifted to Alice. "Who's this?"

"She's with me," I said and placed my fingers in the center of his chest, pushing hard. "You're in our way."

He glanced back at Leon. "Boss…"

Leon nodded. Blackie and another bodyguard, Ron, moved swiftly past me, jerking Alice's arms outward, patting her down.

"Watch it, Mister!" Alice hollered as she yanked her arms from Ron's grasp.

I spun around. "Hey! That's a woman you're frisking! Show some respect!"

"Well, well, lookie here," Blackie said as he pulled open Alice's suitcoat to reveal her shoulder holster. "Dumb Dora's got a pea shooter. I'll take that." He pulled her gun out and aimed it at her. "Don't move, sister."

Alice's face turned scarlet with anger. "I'm not your sister. My name is Alice!"

Blackie and Ron were extremely effective as Leon's watchdogs and that's why I hated them. They were cruel, insolent, and cold-blooded, however, because I was Leon's friend, they knew never to lay a hand on me. Alice, on the other hand, appeared to be fair game.

"Leon!" I spun toward him. "Call your gorillas off my bodyguard!"

Blackie and Ron laughed as though I'd spouted the funniest joke.

Leon Goldman relaxed behind his desk smoking his smelly cigar and drinking a glass of his favorite hooch, a huge grin pasted on his rounded, middle-aged face. He wore a navy, three-piece suit with a red silk tie—hand tailored, of course. He was involved in bootlegging, gambling, and a variety of lucrative illegal activities, earning him the reputation of a prominent "wheeler-dealer" in St. Paul. He also had quite a reputation as a womanizer, even though he had a wife and a couple of adorable kids.

For years, he and my late husband had been fierce enemies, but after Gus' death, Leon and I had come to a truce of sorts, and surprisingly, we'd developed mutual respect for each other. For two people who came from rival camps we got along quite well. That is, when he wasn't teasing me.

Leon rested his cigar in a glass ashtray and chuckled at my hissy fit. "Okay, boys, let her go."

Incensed, I grabbed Alice by the arm and pulled her into Leon's office, shutting the door in Blackie's face.

We sat down on a couple of wooden chairs lining the wall, but Leon gestured with his hand, indicating he wanted us to move closer. "Whatcha doing way over there?"

We scooted our chairs next to his desk.

He held up his liquor bottle. "Would you like a drink?"

We both politely refused.

"So, how's that new husband of yours treating you? I hear you've decided to go into business with Will," Leon said with a chuckle. "A lady detective. Knowing you, that doesn't surprise me."

"Will and I are doing well," I said proudly, "but we aren't working together. I've started my own agency to serve women, and I've already taken on my first case."

"Do tell. Congratulations, sweetheart. Now, what can I do for you ladies," he said, smoothing back his dark, wavy hair. "What's this important issue that's troublin' your pretty little heads today?"

Alice blushed at the compliment.

"I need to hire another bodyguard," I said getting right to the point. "I fired Sean McBride yesterday and Will is adamant that I replace him as soon as possible."

Leon's dark brows knitted together. "Does Will know you're here? The people I associate with aren't the sort you should be depending upon."

"No, he doesn't, Leon—but I'm desperate," I said, knowing the irony wasn't lost on him. When Gus died, I swore I was finished with that world, done with crooked deals and dangerous men. I'd promised myself I would build a new life for me and my son. And yet here I was, asking for help from someone exactly like Gus instead of my new husband. "One of the conditions I agreed to with Will was that I'd always have protection. Now that Sean is gone, Will has put my first case on ice until I hire someone else—someone he personally approves."

Folding his hands on the desk, Leon leaned forward. "What happened with McBride?"

"He's a real heel!" Alice blurted. Realizing she'd spoken out of turn, her face flushed crimson as she cast her gaze to the floor.

"I couldn't have said it better," I said with a cynical laugh. "Sean was arrogant, rude and didn't like taking orders from a woman." I shrugged. "I need someone who will be loyal to me."

"That's a shame," Leon said solemnly. "Never met him myself, but I heard McBride came highly recommended." He picked up his glass and took a sip of his whiskey. "So, what exactly do you want from me?"

"I need to find someone special, Leon. A man who is smart, confident and tough, but who isn't violent—like your guys. The problem is, I have no idea how I'd go about finding someone like that," I said clutching my beaded handbag so tightly my knuckles were white. "But I know you do. You know everyone in the business and you're a good judge of character. I trust your advice."

"The guy would have to be as straight as an arrow," Leon said with a laugh, his generous smile indicating he found my confidence in his judgement flattering. He tossed back the remainder of his drink and stared into his empty glass in thought. "Actually, it's a long shot, but I know someone who just might be a good addition to you and Alice."

My heart fluttered. Could I be this fortunate to find someone so soon? "Who is it?"

"He's about the same age as McBride, but a lot more mature. Do you know Luigi DeLuca?"

My jaw dropped. The DeLuca boys were notorious criminals. "Is he related to the DeLuca family?"

"Yeah," Leon said, reaching for the whiskey bottle to pour himself another shot, "but he's not one of them anymore. They cut him loose when he opposed their way of doing business. Always been a straight shooter—but no fool. It took real gumption for him to stand up to them and walk away."

He tipped back the glass and set it down with a quiet clink. "He's smart, dependable, and honest as the day is long. And he knows everyone in town. He'd be an asset to you, no question about it…that is, if he wants to take on the job."

"He'd have to pass muster with Will," I said, wondering if my husband would give him the nod or send the guy packing.

"Last I heard, Luigi was working in a factory making farm machinery. I'll send one of the boys over to his boardinghouse to have a word with him," Leon said. "If he's interested, I'll send him around to your place to meet with Will. How does that sound?"

"That would be terrific." I rose, eager to go. I needed to get home and have my staff clear out Sean's old room.

"Coming from a family as notorious as his could be a blessing or a curse," I added, "but since you're recommending him, I'll keep an open mind. I've always believed in giving a fellow a fair shake." I leaned across the desk and took his hand. "Thank you, Leon. I appreciate it."

He held my hand a beat too long. "Any time, sweetheart."

Then he pushed back his chair and stood, buttoning his jacket. "I'll see you out."

Leaving Maisie and his paid muscle to stare curiously after us, Leon walked Alice and me out of his office and down the hall to the elevator. "What made you decide to become a detective?" he asked as he pressed the service button.

"I want to help women," I said honestly. "Back when Gus was

alive, he kept such tight control over me that I lived like a bird in a gilded cage. There was no one to turn to when things went south between us, no one I could trust. I want to be *that* person for other women, no matter what kind of mess they're in."

You're a strong woman, Charlotte," he said, nodding in agreement. "You don't tiptoe around what you want—you go after it." He grinned. "Don't shoot the messenger, but you're a lot like Gus. More than you'd ever guess."

The elevator doors opened and Alice and I stepped inside. I had no idea what Leon meant by comparing me to my late husband, but I knew he meant it sincerely. He wasn't the kind of man to flatter a woman with phony compliments. Was I really as fearless and as smart as Gus? Maybe in the nine years we were married, some of his tenacity had rubbed off on me. I certainly needed it to solve this case.

I didn't know what to make of hiring someone who'd once belonged to a dangerous, well-connected family to the underworld. Even if he wasn't one of them anymore, would he be right for me? And more to the point—would he ever be right in my husband's eyes? Common sense told me not to count on it. Even if he *was* the right man for the job, he'd probably refuse the offer.

As the elevator hummed downward, I realized that no matter what, I would have to trust my own judgment—and maybe that was the most Gus-like thing I could do.

Chapter Fifteen

The pendulum clock in the library rang six times. I'd spent all day checking the time, waiting for Luigi DeLuca to arrive to talk to Will and me about the bodyguard position, but he never showed up.

By dinnertime, I decided that he wasn't interested and began to walk the floor, worrying that I wouldn't make it to Marjorie Kimball's on Saturday—two days from now—for our follow-up meeting. I promised I wouldn't call her and risk her husband finding out, but I couldn't stand her up, either. I needed to keep my word. The thought of letting her down gave my stomach the heebie-jeebies.

After dinner, Will went to the den to work on a case while I moved into the sunroom for some solitude to think about my options. Parlor palms, a small table and chairs, and cozy furniture upholstered in yellow damask filled the window-clad room. I often spent time there in the morning with a cup of coffee, reading my mail or browsing Vogue and Harpar's Bazaar.

As I lay on the chaise lounge with a thick blanket over me, I rested my head on a soft feather pillow and stared at the ceiling. There was only one clear answer to my predicament. Will had to accompany me to the Kimball house and wait for me in the car with Alice while I spoke to Marjorie. If he wouldn't allow me to work without two bodyguards, then he had to fill the empty position. I let out a tense breath. Why did everything always have to be so complicated?

I had just dozed off when the telephone in the front hallway began to ring.

Could that be Leon? Or Mr. DeLuca?

False alarm. The calm in Gerard's voice indicated he was speaking to someone he'd talked to before and, frankly, didn't find interesting or controversial. His deep voice droning in the hallway melded into a relaxing blur as I exhaled slowly and snuggled under my blanket.

Heavy footsteps abruptly entered the sunroom. "Pardon me, My Lady," Gerard said in a low voice in my ear, "but Mrs. Rogers is on the telephone and would like to speak with you."

Darn, I thought, *I've got phone extensions all over the house, but not in this room!*

I sat up slowly and pulled back my warm blanket. "Okay, I'll take it in the drawing room." The last thing I wanted to do was stand in the hallway and discuss personal business where everyone could hear me.

In the drawing room, I picked up the telephone and collapsed on the deep blue velvet sofa. "Hello, Ethel."

"Did I disturb you, Char?" Ethel asked sounding concerned. "You sound tired."

"Not at all," I said attempting to sound convincing. "I was just thinking about Marjorie."

"Well, it's not her that I'm calling about," Ethel replied smugly. "I just heard—say, do you have a private line?"

"Yes, I do," I said with a shiver, wishing I'd brought the blanket into the drawing room to keep me warm, "but the darn thing costs an arm and a leg!"

Few people could afford the luxury of a private line, but as far as I was concerned, it was a necessity. As private investigators, neither Will not I wanted our neighbors listening in on our conversations. That was the main reason why I rented private office space to handle my cases.

"I went to dinner tonight with a friend," Ethel said quickly, her voice taking on a conspiratorial tone. "And guess who arrived with a woman on his arm—Matthew Britt!"

I bolted upright. "You don't say…" I let out a disgusted snort. "It sure didn't take him long to forget Eleanor. The man has no shame. Did he bring his new lady to the benefit? I didn't see him with anyone."

"He *met* her at the benefit. According to my friend who is in the know," Ethel continued, "he was sniffing around all the rich, eligible women all night. Not only that, but he's once again throwing money down at the gambling tables like there's no tomorrow. It's absolutely *scandalous*. Betty is probably having heart palpitations over what this is doing to their reputation."

"Do you think he skimmed cash from the benefit?"

Ethel let out a sharp, sarcastic laugh. "Is the sky blue?"

The thought of him spending money meant for the orphanage turned my stomach, and now I wished I'd never gone. I'd donated a generous amount to feed and clothe the children, not to line his greedy pockets. I needed to get the goods on this guy for abandoning Eleanor and see him put away.

"Do you think I should tell Marjorie about this?" I asked, thinking out loud. "It's terribly disrespectful. Those people don't deserve her friendship, but I won't mention it if you think it will only upset her."

"I think it would be better coming from you than me," Ethel said gravely. "This has been a difficult time for her, and I can be abrasive when I'm angry."

I assured her I'd be tactful about it and hung up the telephone. As I shuffled back into the sunroom to grab my shoes, fatigue clouded my thoughts. My arms hung at my sides like heavy weights. I needed to go to bed.

As I entered the great hall, the telephone connected to the guard shack rang in the butler's pantry, a small chamber off the dining room. Its sharp, metallic ring, distinct from the main telephone, was reserved solely for communication between Gerard and the security guard at the property gate. Curious, I followed Gerard to his station and listened to his side of the conversation with Hal, my nighttime security guard.

"You have a visitor," Gerard said, placing his hand over the receiver on the candlestick phone. "A Mr. DeLuca." He glanced at the clock on the wall. "It's rather late for guests. Shall I tell him to return tomorrow?"

"Absolutely not!" His shocked look at my outburst reminded me to calm down and stay focused on this interview. My first hurdle was convincing Will to see him, never mind the hour or Gerard's stiff sense of propriety. "I mean, no, it's not too late—for him, that is. We've been expecting him. Bring him to the library."

With Will on my mind, I swiftly walked to the den, nervous but hopeful, to tell him that we had a visitor. And to prepare him to meet— with an open mind—the black sheep of the DeLuca family.

* * *

"Will," I said quietly as I entered library and walked across the room to the doorway of the den, "someone is here to apply for Sean's position. Leon sent him."

Sitting at his desk, Will looked up from a file he'd been studying. "Leon Goldman? That's not the sort of bodyguard you need, Char. You know what kind of people he surrounds himself with."

"Leon wouldn't send someone unscrupulous to apply for the job," I argued. "He knows me—and you—better than that."

Will and I had previously agreed that he'd hire one bodyguard and I'd hire the other. Since I'd fired his last choice, he'd made it clear to me that he intended to hire Sean's replacement. We never discussed whether I could share in selecting the candidates, but as far as I was concerned, that aspect of the matter was already settled.

Will stood and walked around his desk, meeting me in the doorway. "Who is this fellow? Did Gerard tell you his name? Perhaps I know him."

"Yes, he did," I replied hesitantly. "His name is Luigi DeLuca."

Will's face darkened. "What? You've got to be kidding me. What is this, Leon's idea of a joke? If it is, I don't find it funny."

"Will, please," I said, pressing my hand to his chest to keep him from charging past me to send Mr. DeLuca packing. "At least speak with him before you decide he's unsuitable. All right?"

Gerard's imposing form appeared in the doorway of the library, interrupting us. He frowned in disapproval at the impropriety of receiving a visitor so late. "Announcing Mr. Luigi DeLuca." He stepped aside to admit the man.

Will and I stood speechless, staring at our visitor. He was not what either of us had expected.

"I'm Charlotte Van Elsberg," I said slowly to the man standing in the library doorway as I extended my hand. "I'm pleased to meet you, Mr. DeLuca."

I had envisioned him to be shorter, dressed in overalls with a heavy flannel shirt and a few battle scars, like someone who'd grown up on the streets and now performed heavy work in a factory. I couldn't have been more surprised. And by the surprised look in Will's eyes, I sensed he was taken aback, too.

"Most people just call me Lou," the man said taking my hand. His deep voice had a rich, fluid quality about it, as though he had experience with public speaking. "I apologize for arriving so late. I didn't get word about the job until I got home from work, and it took me a while to get cleaned up and catch the streetcar. I don't own a car."

He appeared to be in his late twenties with dark, penetrating eyes, a permanent five-o-clock shadow and ink-black curls that just brushed the collar of his white shirt. He wore a brown, double-breasted suit, strained across the chest and arms as though he'd borrowed the garment, or the last time he wore it, he was younger and not as well built.

He and Will were the same height. They stared eye to eye as if reading each other's minds. "I'm Will Van Elserg," my husband said, extending his hand.

As they shook, Lou smiled. "I'm honored to meet you, sir. I've heard a lot of good things about you. You're a fine investigator."

Will laughed softly. "It's harder than it looks, take my word for it." He turned and gestured toward the doorway of the den. "After you. We've a good deal to discuss."

I turned to follow them, but Will quietly closed the door in my face.

I stared at the dark oak panel, stunned that my husband would deliberately shut me out of the discussion. My pride stung. I had a good mind to burst in and insist they include me, but I didn't move. Will rarely acted this way, and I knew he didn't do it to upset me. He must have had some tough questions to put to Lou—man to man—and he didn't want me in the middle of it.

"Shall I bring refreshments, My Lady?" Gerard interjected hastily as I turned away from the door.

"We're not to disturb the men, but I'll have something to drink," I said and looked away, distracted. "It's too late for coffee. I'd rather have a Coca Cola."

"Very good, madam." With slight bow and a curt nod, Gerard left the room.

I sat down at the table in the center of the library and waited for the men to reappear. The den's door panel was solid, heavy oak, preventing me from hearing their conversation.

Gerard arrived rather quickly with the soda. My forced smile and extra effort at politeness didn't fool him. His concerned frown indicated he knew Will had upset me. "Would you care for a cheese plate while you're waiting or some of Cook's freshly baked brownies?" he asked gently while pouring the soda into a chilled glass filled with ice chips.

"Thank you, Gerard, but I'm not hungry," I said slowly. "This will be fine."

"Very good, madam." Gerard bowed and left the room.

I sat and sipped my soda, watching the minutes tick by on the wall clock and wondering what was taking the men so long. What were they talking about?

Twenty minutes later, the door burst open and Will emerged with Lou in tow. His serious expression made my heart sink.

He didn't meet your expectations, I thought, bracing myself for disappointment as I stood to receive them. Will had high standards, especially where my protection was concerned.

"Charlotte, meet your new bodyguard," he said in a businesslike tone.

"All right," I said glumly before I realized what he'd said. When the words began to sink in, I blinked. "What did you say?"

Will placed his hand on Lou's shoulder. "Lou is Alice's new partner. I think we should break the news to her tonight as well."

Gerard appeared out of nowhere and announced that he'd fetch Alice. After he left, the three of us walked into the great hall, our voices echoing through the cavernous, two-story room.

"What experience do you have as a bodyguard?" I said to Lou. I needed to know more about the person who would be guarding me.

"I was employed by one of my uncles for years, back when I was involved with my family," he said gravely, his gaze dropping to the floor as if the subject unsettled him. "I left the family business a long time ago, but the work—well, it's second nature to me. It's how I was raised."

"Where have you worked since then?" I asked politely.

"For the past two years I've been employed at the Minneapolis Steel & Machinery Company making Twin City Tractors," he replied. "Before that, I attended the University of Minnesota Law school. I...ah...I didn't finish."

That last comment caused me to do a double take. "Why not?"

"I was in my third year when my father informed me I was expected to serve as his private consigliere to stand between the family and the law," Lou said as we headed toward the servants' stairway. "When I refused, he cut off my tuition. I left school and the family the same day. I knocked about for a few months looking for work before I finally landed a spot on the line at the tractor factory." He shrugged. "A name like mine doesn't open many doors with ordinary folk."

I listened silently, riveted to his story. Now I understood why Leon felt strongly enough to recommend him. Lou had suffered a lot for his principles, losing both his future career and his family. Working at that factory was a dead end for a man with his intelligence.

"I grew up in one of the roughest families in St. Paul," Lou continued. "So, I know the ropes. Did a lot of fighting when I was a kid. Got beat up a lot. Won a lot of fights, too. Violence is never the answer to any situation, but I won't back down if I'm challenged. I know all the families in St. Paul involved in crime and I'm not afraid to stand up to anybody."

We stopped at the top of the stairway to wait for Alice. Lou grinned at me. "I met your late husband, Gus, once—years ago, when Prohibition first got under way. I was out on the town with a few pals, and we tried to buy hooch from him." He chuckled softly. "That fellow was fearless. He scared the living daylights out of me, but he made a deep impression all the same. He told me to leave the booze alone, go to college, and make something of myself. I never forgot it."

I laughed. "Yes, he did have a way with people. That's what made him so successful. It's too bad he chose a life of crime."

Alice suddenly bounded up the stairs, her footsteps tapping with energy on the oak treads as Gerard followed at a measured pace behind her. Her brown eyes widened with curiosity as they rested on Lou.

"Hello," Lou said extending his hand. "I'm Lou DeLuca, your new partner."

She burst into a wide smile, the dimples in her cheeks deepening. "I'm Alice...ah," she hesitated. "Just Alice, okay?"

"Will," I whispered, moving close to my husband as Lou and Alice became acquainted. "Why did you shut me out of the conversation with him? You knew I wanted to be involved in his hiring."

Will cut me a sharp look. "We agreed that you'd hire one bodyguard and I'd hire the other," he said, unsmiling. "I told you before, Char. I won't compromise where your safety is concerned. This was my decision alone."

"But, Will—"

Gerard suddenly approached us. "Shall I show Mr. DeLuca to his room?"

Will turned away from me, letting me know the conversation was finished as far as *he* was concerned. "Not yet, Gerard. Ring Errol and tell him to bring the new Ford around to the carriage porch. I'm driving Lou over to his boardinghouse to pack up his clothes and settle up with his landlord."

Alice's giggling abruptly ceased. "Oh!" she said to Will. "May I come along? I'll drive!"

If I had any doubts about Alice and Lou getting along, one glance proved me wrong.

Alice had stars in her eyes.

Chapter Sixteen

November 4th

"Alice, we need to bring Lou up to date on the case," I said as I paced my office. On my credenza, my new electric percolator rumbled, making my first official pot of coffee in my new office. "I want us to work as a team, so we need to share what we know with him."

I hoped that by doing this exercise, I'd also be able to see things more clearly and perhaps notice something that I hadn't caught before.

Alice and Lou sat in wingback chairs opposite my desk. Alice had taken care this morning to apply a touch of eyeshadow and mascara, bringing out the prominence of her beautiful dark eyes. I'd given her the makeup after I showed her how to use it in St. Cloud. She even wore a dab of red on her lips.

Now, if I could only persuade her to trim a fringe across her forehead and wear the button-pearl earrings I'd given her. It would complete her transformation from the plain farm girl in overalls that I'd hired into quite a looker. But that was for another time. Alice's sharp mind mattered far more to me than her appearance.

I sat down and pulled a legal-sized writing tablet from the bottom drawer. "Here," I said as I leaned across the desktop and handed it to Alice. "You can take notes. Do you know how to type?"

"With two fingers," she replied sheepishly. "I never made it to typing class. I dropped out of school in eleventh grade." She shrugged.

"Pa was gettin' too old for farm work. He needed my help. But I know shorthand!"

"Shorthand?" I repeated curiously. "That might come in handy because I know it, too. In the meantime, I'll buy a typewriter and set it up at the house so you can practice." I reached into the top drawer and pulled out a pencil, handing it to her. "There's a sharpener on the wall by the door."

Alice jumped out of her chair and cranked the metal handle of the rotary device to sharpen her pencil. When she returned to her chair, I instructed her to draw three columns on the page.

"The first column," I said paging through my notes, "is for Dorothy Bloomer."

"Who is Dorothy Bloomer?" Lou asked, leaning back in his chair as he studied us. Will had given him a navy pinstripe double-breasted suit with matching suspenders, a crisp white shirt, and a red-and-white diagonally striped silk necktie. A slight bulge beneath his left arm was the only indication of the shoulder holster he carried. His clothes, dark hair and permanent five-o-clock shadow fit the image of one of Leon's tough men, but Lou had more class in his little finger than Leon's main guard, Blackie, possessed in his entire body.

"She's Eleanor Kimball's friend," Alice offered as she toyed with her long dark braid. "And the leader of a book group that Eleanor attended in St. Cloud."

We'd already given him a brief rundown on the cause of Eleanor's death, her fiancé and her family situation.

"That's where Eleanor met Henry Carpenter," I added, "who owns a publishing house. He and Dorothy were friends. He dropped Dorothy off at the book club one day and was introduced to Eleanor. According to him, it was love at first sight for both and after that, they began a secret relationship." I purposely left off the fact that the autopsy indicated Eleanor was pregnant.

"Is he a suspect?" Lou asked.

Leaning back in my chair, I opened the bottom drawer of my desk and rested my feet on it. "Not at this time. He seemed genuinely distraught by her death."

"Dorothy had a reason to want Eleanor dead," Alice offered. "She was so jealous she could barely see straight. Henry said he'd taken her out to dinner a couple of times. It was only friendship on his part, but Dorothy thought it was more."

"She was uncooperative when I approached her," I said to Lou. "She harbored a lot of anger, but it didn't make sense until I talked with Henry. Plus, Henry told me that Dorothy was supposed to meet with Eleanor the night she died—a fact that Dorothy initially concealed from me. When I approached her about it, Dorothy swore Eleanor never showed up, but she has no one to corroborate her story, giving her a two-hour window to meet up with Eleanor, hitch a ride and force her off the road."

Alice furiously jotted notes in shorthand.

"Column two," I said as the rich aroma of brewing coffee began to fill the air. "Matthew Britt, Eleanor's fiancé. He's admitted to me that he wasn't in love with her, that the marriage was a financial arrangement handled by their parents. His family is broke, and they needed Eleanor's money. Eleanor, or rather her parents, needed the boost in social standing that marrying the son of an ambassador would bring. Matthew's father is deceased, but the family still has powerful connections."

"He found out about Henry Carpenter and confronted her," Lou said. "Am I right?"

"Yes," I countered quickly. "The night she died, they had a huge fight at the Britt residence, but I don't know what time it took place. It could have been earlier in the day, but either way, it gives Matthew a host of reasons to want her dead."

"Jealousy, for one," Lou replied. "Maybe killing her was justice for betraying him. Or, to control the damage to his reputation. With her dead, no one will know about her lover."

"Someone stole Eleanor's diamond bracelet off her arm the night she died and I think it was him," I said, noticing the coffee pot had finished brewing. "Matthew has a gambling problem and a lot of bills keeping up on that huge house he occupies with his mother. I don't know anyone else who stood to benefit as much as he did. That bracelet was worth a king's ransom."

Pushing my desk drawer in, I stood up to attend to the pot.

"Have you checked the local jewelry stores or pawn shops?" Lou asked. "If he pawned it or sold it, the shop owner would have a copy of the receipt."

"Not yet," I said as I poured freshly brewed coffee into three ceramic mugs. "Sean McBride's departure slowed the investigation a bit, but after I meet with Marjorie tomorrow and get her permission to continue, we'll sit down and strategize our next steps."

I handed each of them a steaming mug and sat down again.

"Who is in the third column," Lou asked as he sipped his coffee.

"I don't know yet," I replied, worrying that because I was new at this, I'd missed something important—maybe a lot of things. "We've just begun our investigation."

As I sipped my coffee, I stared at the scattered pile of notes on my desk. Did I have enough information to convince Marjorie that Eleanor's death wasn't an accident? I had no idea, but I was surely going to try. The future of this case depended on it.

*   *   *

November 5th

I awoke early the next morning, unable to shake my apprehension over my meeting with Marjorie Kimball. The biggest issue overshadowing me was whether she knew about Eleanor's 'delicate' condition or not. Did I have the right to divulge this information if she didn't? How would I go about verifying how much she knew without giving it away? I had no idea.

Lillian, my personal maid, chose a navy suit with a white blouse for me to wear to the meeting. The pleated skirt was a modest mid-calf length under a straight-cut jacket. I paired it with a delicate gold necklace and drop earrings.

Standing in front of a cheval mirror, I studied myself critically. I needed to come across as a serious professional. Did I look like a successful female investigator? Exhaling a tense breath, I straightened my collar. As far as I knew, I was the only female private investigator in the Twin Cities, so perhaps I was setting the standard for the women who followed in my footsteps. But then, perhaps all Marjorie cared about was obtaining information on her daughter's accident, not critiquing my appearance.

As I descended the main staircase to the great hall, the sharp tap, tap, tap of a typewriter echoed through the house from the servants' quarters below. Alice was already practicing on the new Olivetti M20 I'd purchased yesterday. Good for her!

Will sat at the round Duncan Fyfe pedestal table with his suit jacket draped over the back of his chair in the small, but cozy breakfast room, drinking coffee and reading the morning edition of the *St. Paul Pioneer Press*. I kissed his cheek as I passed by and took my seat opposite him.

Through the large windows on the east side, dawn was breaking, shooting bright crimson and gold streaks of sunlight through the line of mature oaks at the edge of our property. The uplifting atmosphere was a welcome change from the cloudiness of the past few days, and I hoped it was a good sign for my meeting.

Gerard suddenly appeared at the table and poured me a steaming cup of freshly brewed coffee from a tall, silver coffee pot. "Good morning," he said in his deep English voice. "Would you care for a glass of orange juice, My Lady?"

"Yes, I would, Gerard." I picked up my coffee cup and took a sip, savoring the deep robust flavor. I loved my morning coffee, although this wasn't my first cup of the day. Lillian always served me a small pot of coffee on a breakfast tray every morning in bed.

"I'm glad that Alice is already practicing on her new typewriter," I said conversationally. "I heard her pounding away on it as I came down to breakfast."

"I beg your pardon, madam," Gerard said gently. "I believe that is one of the kitchen maids typing recipes for Cook."

"Oh, my," I said with a surprised chuckle. "I had no idea anyone else would be interested in it. Well, all the staff are welcomed to use it."

Gerard placed the pot on the sideboard and left the room.

"Are you prepared for your appointment today with Mrs. Kimball?" Will asked me without looking up from his paper.

I let out a deep breath. "As much as I'll ever be, I guess."

"You don't sound ready to me," he said flatly as he turned the page.

Whatever courage I had immediately disintegrated. "What is that supposed to mean?"

He looked up. "You sound unsure of yourself. You're not going to get very far with your client if you approach her with an attitude like that." He folded the paper and set it aside. "You need to project confidence."

My shoulders slumped. "How am I supposed to do that?"

"Regardless of your motives for helping people, this is a business, Char," he said as he picked up his coffee cup. "When dealing with clients, upholding professionalism is crucial. It'll make or break your reputation."

"Okay," I said, sounding more confident than the pounding of my heart allowed. If reputation mattered that much to him as a man, I hated to think how much more it would count against a woman. Most men believed women were too emotional to be taken seriously. "I'm listening."

Will drained his cup then stood up and grabbed the coffee pot off the sideboard. "Stay focused on your mission, not your mistakes," he said as he refilled both our cups. "Present only the facts. That's what the client is paying you for, not your opinion—unless you're asked for it. Even then, be careful not to raise their expectations on a hunch. If it doesn't pan out, they'll blame you."

He set the pot back on the sideboard and sat down again. "If the client gets upset at what they hear, don't lose your temper and don't make excuses. Be informative, but don't argue with them. Stay focused on the facts of the case and don't try to calm them by promising something you're not sure you can deliver. The evidence speaks for itself. If it's not what they wanted to hear, it's up to them to deal with it. You're being paid to tell them the truth."

"All right," I said and gripped my coffee cup with both hands to keep them from shaking.

"Make sure you know your facts inside and out," he continued. "Nothing rattles a client more than when you're stumbling through a pile of papers for information that you can't find."

"That's no problem," I said and sipped my coffee. "I reviewed the case yesterday and I'm ready on that score."

The hardest part would be talking to Marjorie about Eleanor's delicate condition. It was a major factor in the case because it could have contributed to someone—specifically Matthew Britt—wanting her dead. I only hoped that Marjorie held as much of an open mind about it as I did.

Chapter Seventeen

"Wish me luck," I said to Lou as he pulled the car to the curb a half-block from Marjorie Kimball's home.

Alice jumped out and opened the door for me. "Do you want one of us to accompany you to the house? I could hang out close by in case you need me."

Grabbing my beaded handbag, I slid out of the car and straightened my clothes. "That won't be necessary. I'll be fine. No one at the Kimball residence would harm me. Mr. Kimball is the only one I need to be careful of and he isn't home."

"Are you sure?" Lou asked boldly. "How do you know that?"

"Marjorie purposely set up the meeting during a time when Robert will be out on the golf course," I replied.

"All right, but we'll keep an eye on the house," Lou said confidently. "If anything looks suspicious, we'll be there for you."

"Absolutely. Thanks." I said goodbye, feeling more confident in my team that I'd had since I started this case, and walked to the Kimball residence; a mansion constructed of pale gray limestone with a red slate roof. As before, I traveled up the front sidewalk to wide steps that led to a stone terrace at the front entrance. I barely reached the top step when James, the butler, appeared at the arched, wrought-iron-and-glass doors and ushered me into the spacious, marble-tiled foyer.

"I have an appointment with Mrs. Kimball," I said to him, remembering to keep my tone cool and assured to project self-confidence, even though my stomach fluttered with tension.

"She's expecting you," James said in a stiff, formal tone as he led me into the sitting room. I sat on one of the cream damask settees and stared out the large windows, taking in the lovely view of the shimmering blue lake across the street. "Mrs. Kimball will be with you shortly," he added. "May I serve you some coffee?"

"Yes," I said politely and clasped my shaking hands, desperate to contain my nervousness.

A silver coffee service sat on the circular mahogany table separating the twin settees. James poured the coffee and set the Limoges porcelain cup with pink tea roses in front of me positioning the handle to the right side for convenience. I picked up the delicate cup and saucer to keep busy while I waited.

As I gazed out the window, a young couple appeared slowly walking arm in arm along the boulevard, laughing and gazing at each other with long, captivated looks. Curious, I watched them for a few moments before realizing that it was Alice and Lou keeping a discreet eye on the house. I smiled at their loyalty. I was the luckiest gal in town!

After a few minutes, Marjorie appeared, her tall, lithe form sweeping into the room in a pale peach dress with a dropped waist. Her makeup, though subtle, had been expertly applied. The finger waves in her pale blonde bob looked freshly styled. Pearl drop earrings adorned her ears. "Charlotte, darling," she said in a slow, breathless voice as she approached me and took my hand in hers. "I hope I haven't kept you waiting long."

"Not at all," I replied with the deepest calm I could muster.

She sat on the settee facing me. James appeared and poured a cup of coffee for her, then silently retreated, leaving us alone.

"You said you'd have answers for me today," she said abruptly dropping all pretense of warmth now that we were alone. "What did you find out? Who was in the car with Eleanor?"

My palms began to sweat. I set my rattling cup on the table and clasped my hands in my lap.

Will's voice suddenly replayed in my head. *Stay focused on the facts of the case...*

"So far, I have identified two people who potentially benefitted by Eleanor's death," I began. "Dorothy Bloomer and Matthew Britt."

Marjorie frowned, her eyes reflecting doubt. "Dorothy Bloomer? What would she gain by Eleanor's death?"

"She was jealous," I said quickly, "of Eleanor's relationship with Henry Carpenter."

Marjorie blinked, staring at me in puzzlement. "Who is Henry Carpenter?"

The confusion on Marjorie's face made my heart thud. She didn't know about Eleanor's affair with him.

I cleared my throat. "Eleanor and Henry were lov—um…close. They had a secret relationship."

The shock that suddenly filled Marjorie's eyes made me wish I hadn't said anything at all. "I…I thought you knew," I said quietly.

"That she and this Henry person were carrying on?" She slowly shook her head, as if in a daze. "I don't believe that."

I suddenly didn't care whether she believed me or not. I'd come here to report everything I'd found and that was what I planned to do. I didn't spend the last week struggling to gather information just to hold back now to salvage her feelings. If she fired me for telling her the truth, so be it. I was determined to do the job she'd hired me to do and that meant telling her everything.

"They weren't carrying on, they were truly in love, and her death has devastated him," I replied honestly. "I saw Henry at the funeral and spoke with him at length this week. Dorothy Bloomer introduced Eleanor to him at a book group meeting, and they began seeing each other in private. Regardless of how it sounds, he wasn't a back door man looking to get his hands on her money. He's a decent person and a very successful businessman. He gave Eleanor that diamond bracelet she always wore. The one that's missing."

Marjorie stared at me wide-eyed as though she found it impossible to comprehend. "You're sure about this?"

"Yes," I said. "As for Dorothy, I haven't confirmed it yet, but she could have been the other person in the car with Eleanor. Dorothy was supposed to meet with Eleanor for dinner the night of the accident. She says that Eleanor stood her up, but she doesn't have anyone to corroborate her story so she could be lying to cover up the two-hour gap in her timeline. She could have met with Eleanor, been instrumental in the crash and taken off on foot. According to Henry, Eleanor was going to quit the book group that night because of Dorothy's jealousy. Dorothy may have taken the bracelet out of spite."

Marjorie stood and walked over to the window, gazing out at the lake across the street. "I knew Eleanor wasn't happy with Matthew," she said with a sniff, "but I had no idea things were that bad." She spun around. "How long has it been going on with her and this fellow?"

"They started seeing each other after the first time Eleanor met with the book group."

Marjorie gasped. "That was six months ago. Why didn't she tell me about it?"

"I don't know," I said, though the answer wasn't hard to guess. Eleanor couldn't bear the thought of marrying that slimy pig, Matthew Britt, and planned to elope with Henry before her family could stop her.

"The only other person I've investigated so far is her fiancé," I said quickly to change the subject. "He had plenty of motive to want Eleanor out of the way." I swallowed hard, knowing I was beginning to tread on sensitive territory. "One of my sources overheard the Britt staff talking about them. I haven't confirmed the time yet or exactly what was said, but Matthew and Eleanor had a heated argument the day she died. If she told him about Henry, he might have wanted her out of the way to preserve his family's reputation. A bereaved fiancé elicits more sympathy than a jilted one." I looked away to keep my courage. "Especially in her condition."

"What?" Marjorie spun away from the window, clutching her hands on the back of the settee as if to keep her knees from collapsing. "What condition—"

"That's enough," Robert Kimball announced in a brisk voice. He strode into the room, a tall, imposing, gray-haired figure in a black suit. Looking straight at me, his ice-blue eyes narrowed menacingly. "This conversation is over and I want you to leave. *Now*." He gazed past his shoulder toward the doorway. "James! Escort this woman out of the house!"

I stood up, stunned by not only his sudden appearance, but his unfounded anger toward me as well. "Why? What have I done?"

Marjorie's fine-featured face paled, her amber eyes widening at his sudden intrusion. "Robert," she said with a gasp. "What are you doing here?"

"I'm taking control of this situation before it gets out of hand," he snarled and pointed at me. "How much money is this charlatan demanding to fill you with lies?"

"I beg your pardon," I said, incensed by his accusation. "I'm not a charlatan and I'm not trying to deceive her. She's asked me to look into the circumstances surrounding Eleanor's death and that's what I've done."

James hurried into the room, eyeing me suspiciously.

"Get her out of here," Robert bellowed at James. "And don't ever allow her in this house again."

His effort to silence me angered me. "I think it's interesting how you appeared just as I was about to reveal the most important information I uncovered about Eleanor to your wife. You've been here the entire time spying on us, haven't you?"

Marjorie moved quickly toward us and placed her hand on my arm to stall James, her face stricken. "What information?"

"Don't listen to her!" Robert shouted, red-faced as he jerked her hand away. "She's a con artist!"

He turned back to me shaking his fist in my face. "And if you utter another word, you'll eat this. Then I'll have you arrested for trespassing."

If he thought he could intimidate me, he was sadly mistaken. Revealing sensitive and possibly hurtful information to Marjorie was difficult because I didn't want to cause her any pain, but standing up to her bully of a husband was right up my alley. I'd survived nine years of marriage to one of the most dangerous men in St. Paul. Robert Kimball's threats didn't frighten me.

"The autopsy report revealed that Eleanor was pregnant," I replied boldly, shoving his fist away. "According to Henry, they were going to elope."

Marjorie's face turned crimson, her response sounding like strangled squeak. "That's not true! How dare you disrespect the memory of my daughter like that? She was a good Christian girl!"

"I'm sorry, Marjorie. I know this is difficult to hear, but it's true," I said as James grabbed me by the arm. I quickly shrugged his hand off. "At first, I debated whether or not to reveal it because I knew it would devastate you, but as her mother, *you deserve to know*."

Marjorie began to sob as she collapsed on the settee. "No, not it's not true. Eleanor would never do that to me…"

Reaching out, Robert shoved me toward his servant, knocking my beaded bag out of my hand and causing me to stumble. I fell against James, pressing my palms on his chest to keep myself upright.

"You've read the autopsy report," I said to Robert as I recovered my balance and snatched my handbag off the floor. "You knew she was pregnant, but you deliberately kept it from your wife. We both know who's really hiding behind lies."

"Get out!"

James grabbed my arm and pulled me into the foyer. He jerked open the wide front door and shoved me out of the house. "Don't ever come back!"

I lurched onto the terrace, nearly losing my footing. Stumbling down the steps, I turned my ankle and began to limp as I made my way along the sidewalk. Suddenly, Alice and Lou appeared, meeting me halfway, each one taking an arm to support me.

"Are you all right, Miz Char?" Alice asked quickly. "We got ya. Lean on us."

I suddenly began to laugh. A charlatan? I'd been called some interesting names in my life but that was not one of them. My ankle hurt like the devil and my ego had been dealt a nasty bruise but my resolve to learn the truth about Eleanor's death had never been stronger. It was going to take more than a few threats from an arrogant louse like Robert Kimball to make me back down.

But how did he know Marjorie and I were meeting today? Judging by the shocked look on her face when he appeared, she hadn't breathed a word to anyone. There was only one other person who knew my plans—Sean McBride. That snake, playing tit for tat. I wondered how much money Robert had paid him to sell me out.

That said, if Robert held back Eleanor's condition from Marjorie, what else was he hiding? And just how far would he go to keep it hidden to protect his reputation? I had no idea, but his behavior made me wonder if he was the mysterious person in the car with Eleanor when it crashed. He certainly had a lot to lose if Eleanor's secret became public and the way he acted today proved that he was willing to do whatever it took to keep it concealed.

Robert Kimball just filled the empty column in my list of suspects.

Chapter Eighteen

Alice and Lou walked me to the car, one on each side holding me up as I limped down the street.

"Are you all right?" Lou asked, concerned. "You nearly took a nasty spill coming down the steps."

"I'm fine," I said even though my ankle was swelling and pressing uncomfortably against the strap of my shoe. "I'm so mad I could spit. That Robert Kimball is a—"

"He was there? You said he would be golfing," Lou said, interrupting me.

Stepping on a pebble, my sore ankle turned again, causing me to shriek as my leg buckled. Lou scooped me in his arms and carried me the rest of the way to the car. Together, they helped me slide onto the seat.

Alice ran ahead and stood by the open car door.

My goodness, I thought as he gently set me down. *Sean McBride would never have shown such chivalry.*

"He was supposed to be golfing, but someone tipped him off," I said as I collapsed in the back seat, wincing from the pain. "Gosh, I could really use an ice-cold Coca Cola about now."

Lou leaned in. "I was thinking more along the lines of a hot brandy when you get home. It'll settle your nerves and dull the pain." He glanced at my shoe. "You'll need to take it easy and elevate that foot for a day or so."

I shook my head at my clumsiness as I exhaled a deep, frustrated sigh. Why did I have to go barreling down that stairway like a cow on a crutch? I didn't have time to rest up. I had a case to solve.

Alice and Lou slid into the front seat and Lou started the car. He put it in gear to take off when I touched his shoulder. "Don't go yet!"

Ivory emerged from the thick, bare hedge separating the neighbor's property from the Kimball estate. Wearing her black uniform, she darted toward the car and circled around to the opposite side, jerking open the door. "I can't stay long. I think I'm being watched."

Crouching, she sat on the running board and leaned inside the vehicle. "The house is in an uproar. As soon as you left, the Kimballs had quite a go-round," she said breathlessly. "Mrs. Kimball accused her husband of betraying her by suppressing the truth. He shouted at her that Eleanor's secrets and her disgrace had been buried with her and that's where they were going to stay. The investigation was over." Ivory placed her hand over her chest and let out a deep breath. "Then Mrs. Kimball said something odd. She said, 'Where were you the night Eleanor's car went off the road? I know you weren't at the club like you said you were.' Then she screamed, 'Where were you?' When he wouldn't tell her, she threw a vase at him and stormed out."

I nodded to show I was listening, but at the same time, my thoughts were charging ahead at full speed. So, he wasn't home the night Eleanor was killed. If he wasn't at the club, where was he? I needed to find out.

"I didn't know about Miz Eleanor's condition," Ivory said with a tear in her eye. "It makes me sad, but now I want you to catch who did this to her more than ever."

She stood up and straightened her dress. "I'd better get back before anyone realizes I'm gone, but before I go, I heard some gossip you might be interested in. I don't know if it's true, but I heard from the kitchen cook that the Britt staff walked out. All of them. They hadn't gotten paid in two weeks."

That's interesting, I thought to myself. Betty Britt had enough money to put on a ritzy fundraiser with fancy canapés, desserts and bootlegged champagne, but not enough to pay her staff.

"Thank you for the information," I said to her. "Call if anything else happens. Do you still have my number?"

"Yes. I will call, I promise." She ran from the car and disappeared behind the lilacs.

*   *   *

Once we arrived home, I hobbled into the house but only made it as far as the sunroom before I collapsed on my yellow Damask lounger. One of the maids saw Alice and Lou assisting me and frantically ran to tell the others that I was injured. Before I could find a comfortable position for my foot to rest, I had a crowd of people peering down at me, wringing their hands over my condition.

"You need to see a doctor," Gerard said gravely as I lay on the chaise lounge, resting. "I'll ring Dr. Daly and see if I can get him to come out here today. You shouldn't be moved."

"Lord almighty," Cook said dryly as she examined me with the concern of a mother hen. "It's a sprained ankle, not a broken neck. I can take care of her. There's no need to bother the doctor. She'll need to rest for a few days, keep that foot elevated, but it'll heal on its own."

Cook, a widow with several grown children, was short and squat with naturally curly hair the color of a fresh carrot. She wore her thick hair in a chignon at her nape, but tendrils of loose natural curls framed her face. She turned to the petite, sniffling maid who'd summoned her. "Lila, fetch a bottle of aspirin and an ice pack. I need to get this swelling down."

Lila ran out of the room.

"I want to go upstairs," I said, knowing it would be a challenge to tackle the grand stairway. "If I have to lay down and elevate my foot, I'd rather be in my bed." I glanced at the doorway. "Is Will home?"

"No, madam," Gerard said as he and Lou lifted me to my feet. "But he's expected soon for lunch."

The men took me up to my bedroom and placed me on the bed. Cook followed behind with the ice pack, and Lillian followed her carrying a tray filled with a glass of iced tea, a small plate of warm ginger snap cookies and an egg salad sandwich on Cook's fresh bread. Plus, the bottle of aspirin for the pain.

Gerard started the fireplace. One by one, everyone went back to their jobs and left me alone to rest.

Since I couldn't do anything else right now, I devoured my sandwich as I flipped through Will's copy of The Saturday Evening Post. I was snacking on a cookie when heavy footsteps pounded on the stairway, bounding two at a time. Will burst through the open door carrying a wooden cane and approached the bed, staring down at my ice-covered ankle. "Hmmm…what does the other guy look like?"

We stared at each other for a moment and burst out laughing.

"It wasn't my fault!" I said through my laughter. "The heel of my T-strap shoe wobbled on a loose pebble of cement and my foot twisted sideways."

Will grinned as he set the cane against the bedside table. "Are you sure Mrs. Kimball didn't spike your tea?"

I dug an ice chip from my water glass and tossed it at him. "If she had, I probably wouldn't be in this mess. I wouldn't have been in such a hurry." No need to tell him that I had James, the Kimball butler, to thank for that.

Will leaned over and wiggled my big toe with a teasing grin. "Nothing seems broken, but it looks like you'll be out of commission for a few days."

Then it hit me. I couldn't investigate Eleanor's murder if I was laid up with a bum foot. Rats!

"I'll be better by tomorrow," I said desperate to assure myself more than him as I glanced at the cane. "I have things to do."

Will leaned over and kissed my cheek. "We'll see." He straightened. "It's up to Cook."

I nearly burst out laughing. *Since when?*

Since the day she moved into my home, Cook had filled the role of caregiver to my staff, dispensing medicine for headaches, indigestion, the flu, aches and pains of every sort. However, she never had to take care of *me* before, and I found it quite restricting.

Will sat on the edge of the bed. "How is your investigation going so far?"

"I have three solid suspects, the jealous best friend, the jilted fiancé, and the abusive father. Each had motive and opportunity, but it's the timing that I'm still trying to work out."

"Well, you're on the right track," he said taking my hand in his. "In my experience, it's nearly always someone close to the victim. Sometimes the answer is right in front of you, but it's so obvious you can't see it."

Will went downstairs to eat his lunch in his office and study a difficult case, leaving me to finish my plate of cookies alone. I didn't feel like reading any longer. Resting against my pillows, I sipped my iced tea, furiously trying to come up with a plan to keep going with the investigation until I could stand on both feet without wincing.

What was so obvious that I couldn't see it? What evidence was I overlooking? I let out a long, slow sigh. This detective business was a lot more difficult than I first thought. Part of me wanted to quit and forget I ever heard of the Kimballs and the Britts. But a still small voice deep in my heart reminded me that if it was easy, everybody would be doing it. That Eleanor's killer would get away with her murder if I gave up. That I'd always regret walking away.

Across the hall, the telephone in my private study rang. After a few moments, Lillian, my maid, hurried into the bedroom.

"You have a phone call. It's a woman, Miss Adams. I wouldn't have bothered you, but she says it's urgent. Shall I take a message?"

"That's Ivory Adams," I said, scrambling to swing my legs over the side of the bed. "Yes, I need to talk to her." I slowly slid off the bed, resting heavily on the cane and my good foot.

"Are you sure you can walk like that without falling?" Lillian asked, her soft voice threaded with concern as she slid her arm around my waist to assist me. "Do you need help?"

"I'll be fine, Lillian. I need to talk to her." Determined to take that call, I slowly hopped into my study using my cane and my good foot and collapsed into the swivel chair. The room used to be Gus' office. The study had a large mahogany desk in the center of the room with a candlestick telephone, brown leather upholstered chairs, and one solid wall of bookcases. A faint aroma of Gus' tobacco still lingered on the furniture and his desk blotter.

Hooking my cane on the edge of my desk, I grabbed the telephone and held the receiver to my ear. "Hello, Ivory," I said into the mouthpiece. "It's Charlotte. Do you have more news about the Britt staff's walk out?"

"I can't talk long," Ivory said, whispering. "I just wanted you to know that this is the last time I'll be calling you. I've just been fired."

"Why? What happened?" I let out a loud gasp as my chair swiveled and banged my sore ankle on the corner of the desk. Ugh!

"Somebody saw me talking to you in the car and snitched to Mr. Kimball." She paused, as though checking on her surroundings. "He told me to get out. I'm supposed to be packing my things."

"Where are you going to go?" I asked, concerned. "Do you have anyone you can stay with?"

"No, ma'am," she said politely. "My family lives in Chicago."

Robert Kimball's callous regard for her service angered me, but at the same time, my heart sank from guilt. I was responsible for her dismissal.

"I have an idea," I said hastily as a plan began to spin in my head, "how would you like to work for me?"

"Yes, ma'am," Ivory replied cautiously. "What position do you have open?"

"Actually, I don't have any," I said, pausing to frame my words carefully. "What I *do* have is a special assignment for you. I want you to approach Betty Britt for a job."

An awkward pause followed my proposal. "Why would I do that? I won't get paid."

"Yes, you will. I'll pay you," I said. "I want you to keep a sharp eye on what's going on over there and report back to me if you notice anything out of the ordinary."

"So, you want me to be a detective—like you?"

I smiled to myself. "Yes, that's exactly what I want you to do. Are you in?"

"Yes, ma'am," Ivory said with a conspiratorial giggle. "This'll be a lark!"

I told her not to breathe a word of our arrangement to anyone and stressed that everything she reported to me was strictly confidential. After she agreed, I said goodbye and hung up the receiver, feeling as though I'd finally found a way to break this case wide open.

Chapter Nineteen

November 6th

By the next morning, the swelling in my foot had gone down a little and the pain had eased, but I still couldn't walk without the cane. My helplessness made me grumpy, restless, and so bored I had to curb my tongue from snapping at people.

My sister, Francie, stopped in before leaving for school to see how I was coming along and to borrow one of my dresses to wear to a birthday party on the weekend. We wore the same size, and it seemed like she spent more time browsing in my closet than I did. I found it annoying that she never wanted to wear her own clothes, but I let her take the dress anyway.

"Cook says you'll be off your feet for a while," Francie said, leaning against the bed with Patches, Alice's kitten, snuggled in the crook of her arm. My sister looked mature for a girl of sixteen in a softly pleated skirt of blue-and-brown plaid paired with a pale blue blouse trimmed with a Peter Pan collar. A brown cardigan rested neatly over her shoulders. "You said you tripped on the steps, but that doesn't sound like you, Char." She frowned and leaned closer. "Come on, what's the real story? Did you get hurt fighting off the bad guys?"

I laughed at her 'bad guys" remark, glad to find some humor in a disappointing situation. "No, nothing as dramatic as that." Looking past her, I glanced through the open bedroom door into the hallway to make sure we were alone before I told her the truth. "I got into an argument with my client's husband, and I made him so angry he had his servant throw me out. I went flying down the front steps and turned my ankle. Twice."

Her eyes widened in surprise. "Oh, my gosh! Did you ruin your shoes?"

"No," I said knowing her concern was because she liked to borrow my black strap pumps. "But the heel tip ripped off one of the shoes so I can't wear them again until I get it fixed."

"I'll do it," she said and stopped stroking Patches' thick fur to hold out her hand. "I'll take it to the shoe repair shop tonight after school, but I need money to pay for it."

I pointed toward a maple chest of drawers. "There is some cash on my dresser. The shoes are in the closet."

Leaving the kitten with me, she went to the dresser and grabbed several bills, noticeably more than she needed. "Oh, and by the way," she said, pivoting toward me as she shoved the money in her pocket, "can I borrow your black rhinestone hair clip to wear to the party?" She slid her finger above one ear, nestling it into the curve of a neat, marcel wave in her chin-length flaxen hair to show me where she wanted to place the clip. "It's the latest thing."

"Okay," I said, losing patience, "but return it to my dressing table box after the party. And I want it back in *one piece*."

"Of course I will, silly," Francie quipped as she patted the kitten on my lap and breezed past me toward my walk-in closet. She stopped suddenly in the doorway and spun around, raising one brow. "Hold on a tick. A servant shoved you down the stairs? Your client's husband must be a real cad. Does that mean you're fired?"

"He tried to fire me, but he didn't hire me," I replied, still sore over Robert Kimball's high-handed attempt to give me the bum's rush. "Until Marjorie shows me the door, I'm on the case."

Francie disappeared into my closet, leaving me to mull over my present circumstances. I was determined to get to the bottom of things for Marjorie. I had rattled her with the news of Eleanor's condition, but that only made concluding the matter even more pressing.

Flopping back against the pillows, I stoked the sleeping kitten's soft fur and exhaled a deep sigh of frustration. Just my luck! The case was on hold again and all I could do was stew while the answers I needed danced out of reach.

*   *   *

Lillian and my nanny, Gretchen, brought the children to the bedroom to spend time with me before their morning nap. It cheered me a little but didn't change the fact that I should be out on the street instead of lounging in bed.

After lunch, Ivory called to say that Betty Britt had hired her yesterday on the spot and put her immediately to work.

"There isn't an ounce of food in the kitchen," Ivory complained. "The staff raided every cupboard to get what they could to make up for their lost wages. I don't fault them, but I got so hungry last night I had to walk to the grocers to buy bread and cheese out of my own pocket."

Sitting at my desk, I tapped my pen on the blotter, wondering where Betty was getting *her* meals from. "How are you supposed to cook without food?"

"I called the grocer today to place a small order to tide me over until Miz Britt hires another cook, but when he found out where the food was to be delivered, he stated no credit—only cash on delivery," Ivory said. "Miz Britt went to the Minneapolis Women's Club for lunch so I can't ask her for the money until she returns."

"Would you like me to send over some food to tide you over until your order is delivered? I'll make sure my staff is discreet."

"Don't worry about me. I'll be fine. I really didn't call to complain. I've got some juicy news for you," Ivory said, her voice heavy with excitement.

"Already?" I asked, amazed. "That was fast. You just got the job yesterday afternoon."

"It happened this morning when I was cleaning Master Britt's study," Ivory said. "First, I found all the pictures with Miz Eleanor torn up in the trash. He simply ripped them up and threw them away!"

"He sounds, bitter," I replied. "Doesn't he?"

"Then, I looked under the cushions of the sofa for loose change and found a gold money clip with a lion's head on it," Ivory said. "It had over five hundred dollars in it! Coins are considered 'finders-keepers,' but that clip held a small fortune and I'm no thief. I gave it to Miz Britt and told her where I found it. She said she knew who it belonged to and that she'd take care of it. She didn't even thank me."

I couldn't understand how this applied to my case, but I didn't say so. "Did she tell you who the owner was?"

"She didn't have to," Ivory responded quickly. "After she dismissed me, I heard her pick up the telephone, so I went to the nook in the hallway and listened. She called Mr. Kimball!"

I bolted upright in my chair. "Robert Kimball? What was he doing at the Britt's house?"

"I was surprised by that myself because he can't stand her. Calls her a nasty old battle-ax. And the feeling must be mutual because Miz Britt told him the clip was empty when she found it," Ivory exclaimed, her voice rising. "She stole his money!"

Good heavens! Was Betty Britt so desperate for cash that she'd steal from Robert Kimball and then lie about it? Or was it to settle a score between them?

"He said he'd send someone over to retrieve the clip," Ivory continued, "but she told him the only way she'd give it back was if he returned the engagement ring at the same time. He made some excuse that she had to talk to Miz Kimball about that. He didn't know anything about it."

Shaking my head, I let out a wry chuckle. "How convenient.

When in a pinch, blame the wife."

"But then she said something odd," Ivory added, piquing my curiosity. "She told him, 'Matthew and I are the only people who know you were here the night of Eleanor's accident. If you don't want that information to land in the wrong hands, I suggest we come to a mutual understanding.' He flew off the handle and said, 'Don't try to strong-arm me with blackmail or you'll end up dead like her.' Then he slammed the receiver down."

This new revelation made my thoughts spin. If Robert had been present at the Britt home the night of Eleanor's death then he knew Eleanor was ending her engagement to Matt. He was probably a witness to their argument. Why was he protecting this information? What was he hiding? If he had been with Eleanor when the car crashed, then he had taken the bracelet. I wondered what he had done with it.

I thanked Ivory for calling me and hobbled back to bed, planning my next move. At least my brain still worked! I needed to start looking for Eleanor's bracelet before the trail went cold. Lou mentioned checking pawn shops and jewelry stores to see if someone had sold it. That was the only lead I had, but if I didn't move fast, Eleanor's bracelet would slip through my fingers, and someone would get away with murder.

*   *   *

November 7th

The next morning, after getting dressed, I hobbled into my closet and found a pair of flat shoes in soft leather with a single strap across the instep. I brought them back into my bedroom, slipped on a pair of wool knee socks and squeezed my bad foot into one shoe. It was a tight fit, but workable.

Ignoring Lillian's protestations, I swore her to secrecy then sent her downstairs to summon Alice and Lou to my study. A few minutes later, they burst through the door as though their tails were on fire.

"What's going on?" Lou asked, breathless from bolting up the stairs. "Are you okay?"

"No," I blurted, sitting behind my desk. "I've got to get out of here before I go off my rocker. We're going to the office, but we need to act quick before Cook finds out. She thinks I need more time to recover."

"I'll get the Tin Lizzy," Lou said with a conspiratorial grin and dashed out.

"I'll help you downstairs," Alice said as she grabbed my arm.

I stood up and gently pulled away. "I'll be fine. Go downstairs and get my coat and scarf out of the closet before Gerard finds out what's going on. He'll tell Cook!"

Alice reluctantly left me, but as soon as she disappeared, I left my desk and walked—without a cane—out of my office and down the stairs. At first, my ankle hurt like the devil, but the more I walked on it, the easier stepping became. Alice met me at the bottom of the stairs and slid my coat over my arms. I already had my snug, bell-shaped cloche hat on so I quickly buttoned my coat and donned my gloves as we hustled to beat the band out the front door to wait for Lou. It felt ridiculous to sneak out of my own house, but my husband and my staff hovered over me so much that I had no other choice.

We stood on the steps inside the carriage porch in the brisk November air waiting for Lou. Along the edge of my property, the bare oaks were massive and stately, their branches outlined against a pale gray sky. I shivered as an icy breeze ruffled the edges of my hair.

Before long, I heard the familiar rumble of the engine as Lou drove the Ford out of the garage and up the driveway to the house. Lou pulled inside the carriage porch, we got in, and the car rolled away. I waved to Chet, my daytime security guard, as he opened the gates for us and we were off.

"Where to?" Lou asked as he pulled onto Summit Avenue.

I pulled a lap robe over my legs to keep me warm. "Big Louie's for lunch! I'm dying for an ice cream sundae. Then we'll go to the office. We need to complete our list of suspects."

I owned several ice cream shops that Gus had acquired to use the backroom and basement to store his bootlegged liquor, but Big Louie's had always been my first choice. The workers were friendly, the place carried the pungent aroma of freshly roasted beef and hearty soups, and the ice cream was so rich and sweet it practically melted in my mouth.

The little shop had a tin ceiling and a soda fountain with a marble counter that served sodas, phosphate drinks, milkshakes, lemonade, coffee and hot chocolate. We sat in a wooden booth and savored the daily luncheonette special of vegetable beef soup and a ham salad sandwich. Around us, the clink of spoons against glass sundae dishes mingled with the chatter of customers, giving the place a warm, bustling, home-style charm.

For dessert, we had turtle sundaes, a lot of laughs, and steaming cups of coffee.

Then we drove to the office, plugged in the percolator, and got down to business.

"Robert Kimball," Alice said as she sat in her chair facing my desk poised with her pad and pencil. "He's a nasty one."

"And a man with a lot of secrets," I added. "He knew about Eleanor's pregnancy so he must have seen the autopsy report. A fact that he withheld from Marjorie."

"He found out from Sean McBride that Miz Kimball hired you and ambushed your meeting," Alice stated as she jotted the information in shorthand. She looked up. "Instead of throwing you out, the coward told his butler to do it."

"Then Ivory risked everything to meet us at the car," I said solemnly. "She reported that Marjorie and Robert got into a fight after I left, and that Marjorie demanded to know where Robert was the night Eleanor died."

I sat back in my chair and folded my hands. "Well, I know where he was. Ivory is now working for Betty Britt. She called yesterday and said that Robert was at the Britt's house the night Eleanor died. Robert, Betty, Eleanor and Matthew were there. She found out because Robert's money clip fell out of his pocket and landed between the sofa cushions in Matthew's study. Then Betty called Robert and tried to bribe him for her silence. He said if she tried to strong-arm him, she'd be dead like Eleanor."

Alice and Lou stared at me, speechless.

"So, if Robert was with Eleanor that night, and he was the other person in the motorcar, then he left his own daughter to die," I said gravely. "I wonder if he took the bracelet because it tied Eleanor to her lover."

"Or...he could have given it as an extravagant gift to his mistress," Lou said bluntly.

Alice blushed.

I stared at him in wry amusement. "That old goat?"

"Take it from me," Lou added with a grin, "a wealthy, high-handed fellow like that always has one."

"So," I said with a shrug, "first thing tomorrow, we start hitting the pawn shops and jewelry stores to find out if one of our suspects pawned that bracelet. Fair enough?"

"Okay!" my team said in unison.

I held out my hand. One by one, in the center of my desk, we stacked our hands together in a show of solidarity. The hunt for Eleanor's bracelet was on.

Chapter Twenty

November 8th

The next morning, my best-laid plans to search for Eleanor's bracelet were foiled by the one force I couldn't argue with—Mother Nature. I woke up to a huge snowstorm sweeping across the Midwest. Heavy winds blowing sticky snow grounded my quest indefinitely.

I spent the day wandering about the house, staring out the window at the untimely blizzard and complaining. Even Patches, Alice's sweet calico kitty, jumping into my lap with a loud purr, couldn't completely deter my disappointment and restlessness.

Enough with the delays, I thought grumpily. *If I don't get on with this search, the trail won't just get cold but completely disappear.*

If that beautiful bracelet landed at a prestigious place like J.B. Hudson Jewelers, it could already be resold. I'd promised Henry that I'd find out what happened to it and I couldn't let him down. The depth of his grieving broke my heart and though I couldn't bring her back, I could at least give him closure on one small piece to hold in place of her.

* * *

November 13th

The storm lasted for two days, dumping eighteen inches of snow across the state, It took another two gloomy days for Public Works' road crews to get the streets cleared. But on the fifth morning, to my relief, the sun returned, casting a brilliant blue sky over the glittering drifts.

After a hot breakfast, I dressed in my dark green wool suit, tugged on thick stockings, and buttoned myself into my wool-lined boots, steeling myself against the cold as we set out to make the rounds from shop to shop in search of a break in the case.

"I'll see to the pawnshops," Lou said, easing the motorcar onto Summit Avenue heading for Minneapolis. Huge snow piles lined the side of the road where it had been pushed aside. "Those places aren't fit for ladies."

"That sounds like a great suggestion," I replied from the backseat as I tucked my wool blanket around my legs. "Alice and I will visit the jewelry stores."

My first jewelry store visit ended as quickly as it began. After stepping over a huge pile of snow at the curb, I stomped the snow off my boots at the door. The bell above the door jingled, heralding our arrival as Alice and I went into a small, family-owned shop. The narrow store had one long glass case stretching from the entrance to the back wall filled with dozens of glittering specimens.

A tall, slim elderly gentleman with thinning gray hair and gold, wire-rimmed glasses emerged from the doorway of his workshop. He wore a long cotton work apron over a white shirt, dark vest and trousers. "May I help you ladies?"

"Yes," I said politely. "I'm looking for a diamond line bracelet." I held out my wrist, showing him one with sparkling baguette stones that I'd received for my last birthday. "Similar to this, but with larger stones."

He examined the one on my wrist. "That's a beautiful piece." He looked up. "What size diamonds are you looking for?"

I smiled. "Half-carat, emerald cut in a platinum setting."

He frowned as though he doubted I understood the cost of what I was shopping for.

"I don't have anything that exclusive," he said hesitantly. "I can certainly make one for you, but it would require a sizeable down payment."

Disappointed, I shook my head. "I don't have the time that a special order requires. I need it as a gift for my mother's birthday party this weekend."

Jeepers, that lie slid right off my tongue like melted chocolate off a spoon. I was getting good at this business of tailoring my story to suit the occasion. Maybe, too good, though. I didn't want to start believing my own fibs!

The jeweler attempted to interest me in another piece, but I declined politely, then thanked him and left the shop with Alice in tow. The next jewelry store yielded the same result. And the next. And the next. My enthusiasm started to wane.

The morning's unfruitfulness revealed another aspect of investigating that, in my naiveté, I hadn't anticipated when I decided to reinvent myself and step into the *glorious* job of sleuthing—the long, arduous grind of looking for a needle in a haystack. Spending hours, sometimes days, pounding the pavement without a single new lead or tangible results. How did Will handle this without getting discouraged?

By late afternoon, my feet were frozen, my smile ached, and the shine had worn clean off the adventure, but we'd covered every jewelry store and pawn shop in Minneapolis.

"What do we do now?" I mumbled glumly aloud, more to myself than my companions, as we sat in a scarred wooden booth at Big Louie's soda shop, devouring ice cream sundaes and sipping on strong black coffee.

"We go home, get some rest and start again tomorrow," Lou said, scraping his spoon along the bottom of his tulip glass to capture the last bit of vanilla ice cream smothered in dark chocolate and roasted almonds. "We'll get out the telephone directory and start working the pawn shops and jewelry stores in St. Paul."

He and Alice sat side by side across from me, a circumstance that wouldn't have occurred in a million years with Sean McBride. The difference between Sean and Lou came down to two simple attributes: manners and values.

A girl from a hard-scrabble upbringing who had learned not to presume too much, Alice treated Lou with quiet patience, never raising her voice nor offering the smallest criticism. Yet there was a reserve about her, as though she remained unsure of his feelings and uncertain of her own place beside him.

Lou, for his part, treated her with respect and singular attentiveness that surprised me. He listened to her when she spoke. He noticed when her coffee needed refilling. He opened doors for her and treated her like a respectable woman rather than just another hired gun. It wasn't a grand romance, at least not yet, but something tender was slowly unfolding between them and I hoped that when it did, Alice wouldn't end up with her heart broken.

*   *   *

November 14th

The next morning, we resumed our search again, this time in St. Paul. As before, we struck out repeatedly. But just before lunch, our big break came—with more roadblocks.

"I found it," Lou said as he climbed into the Ford, grinning from ear to ear. "Someone pawned it two days after the accident."

Alice cheered.

My heart soared. "How much do you need to redeem it?" I asked eagerly and opened my clutch to count out the money.

He let out a long sigh. "Well, it's not that simple. You need the original ticket to get it out of hock and since we don't know who holds it, we can't go after it."

"But…but…it was stolen from a crime scene," I sputtered. "Did you tell the pawnbroker that?"

"Yes, but he won't budge," Lou replied with a shrug. "Without the ticket, we have to wait thirty days, and if the ticketholder hasn't redeemed it, then we can purchase it."

"We can't afford to wait that long," I argued. "We need it now.

And if the person who holds the ticket buys it back, we'll never see it again."

I shoved my cash back into my clutch and threw the blanket off my lap. "I'm going into that pawnshop, and I *will* get that bracelet plus the information we need. I'm not leaving here without it!"

Lou jumped out of the Ford and opened my door, clasping my hand to steady me as I slid out. Armed with nothing but female determination, I tromped through the snow and marched into the shop with Alice and Lou behind me, finding myself inside a cramped, dimly lit room. Shelves and glass cases overflowed with tarnished heirloom silver, trinkets, and musical instruments. Mustiness and stale cigarette smoke tainted the air. In one case, I noticed a hand-painted porcelain figurine of a nightingale under a glass dome. It looked so life-like, I was tempted to buy it.

The pawnbroker, a short, balding man with a round stomach and a heavy black mustache stood behind a thick glass jewelry case, eyeing me suspiciously. A window in the front of the shop cast a golden stream of sunlight across his gray, pinstriped shirt and dark suitcoat. Dust motes swirled around him like a cloud of tiny fairies dancing in a frantic frenzy. An enormous glass ashtray brimming with cigarette butts sat on the case, bitterly assaulting my nostrils.

"Afternoon, ma'am," he said in a deep, cautious voice. "What can I do for you today?"

"I'm here about that diamond bracelet that my colleague inquired about," I said, getting my little speech started.

"As I told your *colleague*," he countered gruffly, leaning his elbows on the case, "no ticket, no bracelet. Is that clear?"

I stepped forward, getting as close as I could without touching it and placed my business card on the greasy, worn glass. "It was stolen from an accident scene that I'm investigating, and I can describe it perfectly. A diamond line bracelet set with half-carat emerald-cut stones in platinum. The person who took it was involved in the accident but fled the scene before the police arrived."

He stared at me skeptically. "Sad story. Got proof?"

I eyed him back. "Yes. Does the name Eleanor Kimball sound familiar? Her accident made the front page of the newspaper a couple of weeks ago."

"Like I said, lady, sad story, but not my problem. Obeying the law is my problem. It's illegal to sell the bracelet to someone other than the ticketholder for thirty days. So come back then, and if I've still got it, we'll make a deal."

I opened my purse. "And if I made it worth your while?"

He let out a loud belly laugh. "You trying to bribe me? Is this a trap? You working for the cops? If you are, you're not very good at it."

"No," I said unamused, "I'm working for Eleanor's mother, but if you need more proof, I can come back with her and the cops to get the bracelet because it's *stolen* property."

"Evidence, lady," he bellowed. "I need evidence!"

I glanced around. "Do you have a telephone? I'd like to make a call. I can make it from here or the police station, whichever you prefer."

He nodded toward a doorway in the corner. "In the back room, but not without me present."

"Of course," I said briskly. "I wouldn't dream of making this call without you present."

He led me to a room so small that only he and I could fit inside. A battered metal desk sat against one wall. Metal file cabinets and a massive, free-standing safe lined every inch of the other three walls. Piles of merchandise stacked precariously covered the tops of the cabinets.

He pushed the candlestick telephone toward me.

Handing my clutch to Alice, I picked up the nicotine-smelling telephone and called Marjorie. I told her I'd found Eleanor's bracelet and where, but I couldn't buy it back because the shop owner needed proof that the bracelet was stolen. She gave me a terse answer and hung up.

"Well, now that we have that settled," I said cheerily, "do you mind if we browse while we wait for our proof?"

The shopkeeper narrowed his eyes at me and pulled back the lapel of his coat, revealing a shoulder holster and revolver under one arm. "Don't try no funny stuff, lady, or I swear, I'll throw the three of you out on your ear."

"I assure you," I said holding up my hands in a truce, "everything will be straightened out in a few minutes."

He led us back into the store where I stood browsing the jewelry case for a gift for Francie. I decided on a pair of pearl cluster earrings. I stood counting out the purchase price when suddenly, the screech of a police siren pulling up in front of the store stopped us all in our tracks. Within moments, a pair of officers walked in.

"Mr. Finkel," a tall, dark-haired officer said with authority as he approached. "I understand you're in possession of a stolen bracelet."

Mr. Finkle's round face and neck turned florid, his eyes widening with shock. "Wha-what's going on? Stolen jewelry? Everything's above board here. I don't know anything about some pinched loot."

"Mrs. Marjorie Kimball reported to us that her late daughter's bracelet is in your possession," he said and turned to Lou, ignoring me. "Did you verify this?"

"I didn't actually see it," Lou spoke up. "He said it's in his safe, but when I described it to him, he admitted that someone had pawned it about two weeks ago. It's a unique bracelet worth a small fortune."

"I'm here on behalf of the family," I said to the officer. "I spoke with Marjorie a few minutes ago and told her it was here."

"Mrs. Kimball is on her way to verify that it's the piece that was stolen from her."

I barely had time to digest his words when Marjorie swept into the shop in a full-length mink coat with a wide, shawl collar, presenting herself with all the glamour of a film star. Diamonds glittered from her ears. An invisible mist of Chanel perfume swirled around her like an aura. "Charlotte, darling, is it true? You've found Eleanor's bracelet?"

Mr. Finkel cleared his throat, straightening immediately. "M— Mrs. Kimball, I presume?"

Marjorie turned to him with a beautiful, disarming smile. "Yes. I'm so grateful for your assistance, Mister…"

"Finkle," he said, mesmerized by her charm. "Samuel Finkle, at your service. I'll retrieve the piece for your inspection." He disappeared into the back room and reappeared in a short while with a wooden box. He set the box on the counter and opened it, revealing a half-dozen beautiful bracelets set with various gems.

Marjorie peered at the box and gasped. "That one!" She pointed to a silver bracelet with square diamonds and a break in the links. Mr. Finkel picked it up and placed it in her hand as her eyes filled with tears. "My dear, dear Eleanor…"

The bracelet, once the center of my attention, now slid from his fingers into hers. I let it go. What mattered more to me right now was the ledger behind the counter, worn and handwritten, a potential key. My pulse quickened as I imagined the name scrawled beside the bracelet's entry. Was it Dorothy Bloomer or Matthew Britt? Or Robert Kimball? The person who had pawned it was the thread that would unravel everything and solve this case.

"Mr. Finkle," I said, "may I have the name of the person who pawned the bracelet?"

"Of course," he said quickly, flicking a nervous glance toward the police as he opened the ledger, scrutinizing the pages to find the entry.

I stepped closer, my gaze scanning the rows of scrawled names and numbers, excited that Mr. Finkel, for all his gruffness, was about to show me more than he realized.

"Here," he said, his finger stopping at an entry. "This one. Don't recall the person so my son must have handled it. Can't ask him about it, though. Joe is in Chicago on his honeymoon."

Alice, Lou and I all craned our necks to read the name. I blinked and stared at Lou then at Alice. They looked as baffled as me.

"M. Alsobrook," Alice said aloud. "Never heard of such a person. Have you?"

Marjorie frowned at me, indicating the name didn't mean anything to her.

Obviously, it was fake. One step forward, two steps backward. I stared at the name again, struggling to conceal my frustration. Real detective work was about as easy as shoveling snow.

Chapter Twenty-One

November 16th

Brrring! Brrring!

The shrill cry of the telephone in my study cut through the peaceful hush of night, waking Will and me. And most likely, my entire household.

"What the devil…" Will said in a muffled voice as he turned over in bed, slinging one arm above his head.

Half-asleep, I lifted my head off the pillow and squinted through the dark at my clock on the bedside table. The faint green glow on the clock face read 1:25 in the morning.

Brrring! Brrring!

Will threw off the covers and sprang from the bed, yawning loudly. "I need to get that before it wakes the children."

Assuming it was one of his clients, I closed my eyes again and buried my face deep into the softness of my feather pillow. My mind slipped into a relaxed state, ignoring the heavy thud of Will's bare feet charging across the hall into my study. Will's voice blurred into the night as I snuggled under the covers with a long, rested sigh.

"It's for you," Will whispered suddenly in my ear. "Charlotte, wake up." His wide hand pressed against my shoulder, gentle but insistent, shaking me awake. "There's been an emergency at the Kimball house."

My eyes flew open. "What?" Startled, I lifted my head off the pillow again, blinking the sleep from my eyes. "What did you say?"

The pull chain on the Tiffany lamp on my bedside table jingled, and gradually, a soft, amber circle of light shone in my eyes.

"Marjorie Kimball is on the phone and she sounds hysterical," Will said, leaning over me. "Something has happened over there, but I couldn't get her to calm down and tell me what's wrong."

"Okay," I said throwing off the covers and sitting up. "I'll find out what's going on."

Sliding my legs off the bed, I dropped my feet to the cold wood floor, sending a shiver through my body. I stood up and grabbed my thick, winter robe, hastily jamming my arms into it as I stumbled into my study.

Loud sobs echoed from the receiver lying on the desk. I picked up the telephone and pressed the metal earpiece, icy cold, against my ear. "Hello, Marjorie?" I said in a muffled voice as I spoke into the mouthpiece. "What's wrong?"

"Charlotte, something dreadful has happened. Someone broke into our house!" Marjorie screamed at me.

"Calm down, Marjorie," I said gently as I collapsed in my desk chair. I grabbed a pen and pulled out a notepad. "Take a deep breath and tell me what happened."

"We just arrived home from an evening with friends when we found the French doors in our bedroom ajar," Marjorie replied with a loud sob. "Someone climbed the trellis to the balcony and jimmied the lock in the door to get in. He took all my jewelry!"

"Did you call the police?" I asked, jotting notes on my pad. "Are they on their way?"

"No, Robert won't permit it. He won't allow the scandal to sully our name. He claims he knows who broke in and plans to handle the matter himself using a private firm, if necessary."

A private firm? According to Gus, that meant sending thugs to recover the stolen goods and to teach the offender a lesson he soon wouldn't forget.

"Charlotte, I need you here," Marjorie burst out. "I don't care what Robert's planning. Please, come—now! I don't want any more trouble. I just want my jewels back and I want *you* to get them for me."

I stared at my notepad, stunned. Me? Track down a jewel thief and demand he return her property? What about my primary focus of identifying the person in the car with Eleanor the night she died? Did that just get shoved to the back burner?

The last thing I wanted was to upset Marjorie further, but also, I didn't want to cross Robert's *private* goons and find myself in a perilous situation. And speaking of serious dilemmas, I certainly didn't want to come between Robert and Marjorie again. I'd already done that once and ended up tossed out on my ear. I sighed. What a mess!

"I'm on my way," I said to Marjorie, hoping I could find a way to satisfy her demands without stepping on Robert's toes. "I'll be there as soon as I can." I disconnected the call and set the telephone back on my desk.

The deep, guttural sound of a man briskly clearing his throat jerked me out of my thoughts. I looked up to find Lillian and Gerard standing in the doorway clad in their chenille robes and matching slippers, a Christmas gift from me and Will. Lillian frowned with worry, but Gerard's thick dark brows drew together with unmistakable disapproval.

"There has been an emergency," I said tightly and rose from my desk. "I must go out. Tell Alice and Lou to get dressed and bring the car around."

They silently parted to let me through as I left the room and headed for the bedroom to explain the situation to Will. Any hope of a peaceful sleep in my comfy bed would have to wait.

In the Kimballs' world, peace proved short-lived. Stolen jewels, simmering secrets, and flaring tempers provided fodder for another chapter in a tempestuous marriage that never stopped unfolding. I went into the bedroom to change and brace myself for more of their family drama. Tonight's crisis promised yet another twist in their gilded, tumultuous story.

*   *   *

Within an hour, I stood on Marjorie's front doorstep with my bodyguards in tow, anxious to get to the bottom of things. My breath billowed in small, pillow-like puffs as I stood in the chilly November evening air, bundled up in my long wool coat and cloche hat. Above, heavy clouds were moving across the evening sky. In the distance, the methodic rumble of a late-night freight train rolled along Kenwood rail corridor like an ominous sign. When James finally answered the door, his eyes widened at the sight of my entourage,

"Marjorie is expecting me," I said brusquely and brushed past him, slipping out of my coat and hat. I wasn't taking any chances this time. If Robert decided to take his temper out on me, he'd have to go through my team first. I had no intention of taking any guff from him, but I also didn't want to run the risk of another sprained ankle.

Without waiting for James to announce me, I barged into the sitting room. Marjorie and Robert were seated on opposite settees facing each other, or rather—*facing off*—each holding a stiff drink.

"Charlotte, darling," Marjorie said breathlessly, and set down her gin rickey. Puffy eyes and smeared mascara marred the delicate, high cheekbones of her beautiful face. She sniffled, as though she'd been crying. Her blonde finger waves were mussed from anxiously running her fingers through her hair.

She stood slowly, her usual radiance and elegance replaced by worry and strain. She wore a knee-length, gold chemise of silk tulle, trimmed with layered, diagonal rows of soft ruffles, the perfect dress for socializing and dancing until dawn. According to Ethel, Marjorie employed a French dressmaker who fashioned her wardrobe after the latest Parisian trends. The gown served as a testament to her wealth and social standing, but even the rich couldn't escape life's complications.

"I'm so glad you're here!" She sniffed loudly and pressed a balled-up handkerchief to her lips.

Wearing a black suit and tie, Robert raised his glass of amber-colored liquor and quickly tossed it back. "You two, leave!" he shouted, pointing a finger at Lou and Alice.

"No, they came with Char, so I trust them," Marjorie snapped. "They stay!"

"I'll not allow cheap muscle in my house. Out!" Robert slammed his crystal, lowball glass on the low, circular mahogany table centered between them. "James, throw them out. Now!"

"It's all right, Marjorie," I said interrupting her as she was about to argue with him again. "They'll wait by the front door." I glanced at Lou who studied me intently for instructions. "*Inside* the door. It's cold outside."

"Fine," Marjorie replied, sounding satisfied that she'd won this round. "Come upstairs with me. I'll show you the damage *he* did."

"Who is *he*?"

She stopped and turned back. "Who do you think? That low-class, two-bit thief, Matthew Britt! His sloppy signature is all over my things."

I followed her into the marble-tiled foyer past Lou and Alice, now standing like sentinels at the front door. We went up the sweeping dark oak staircase with wide steps and a curving banister all polished to a soft sheen. Overhead, a cut-glass crystal chandelier scattered warm light across cream-colored walls.

On the second floor, she led me down the hallway into the master bedroom. "There," she said pointing to a set of tall, east-facing French doors that led out to a balcony large enough for two chairs. "He jimmied the latch and entered here so quietly my servants never suspected a thing."

"So, it wasn't locked," I stated, examining it.

Marjorie shrugged. "It's the second floor. " We didn't think it was an issue. Until now."

Nodding, I glanced around and saw nothing else amiss. Besides French doors and a dark hardwood floor, the room contained a large, stately bed with a matching upholstered headboard, dressed in pale linens so perfectly smoothed they looked scarcely slept in. Matching bedside tables and lamps completed the ensemble. To my right, a sitting area contained light blue armchairs and occasional tables arranged on a round, ivory and powder blue Aubusson rug.

"He did all the damage in here," Marjorie said, leading me into a large walk-in closet.

I stared at the carnage, my anger building at the thief's destructiveness—seemingly done out of pure spite. Beautiful dresses had been pulled down and strewn across the wood floor in heaps, presumably in search of a hidden wall safe. Shoe racks were upended, hat boxes opened and dumped. Cosmetics and hair accessories were randomly spilled on Marjorie's lighted vanity.

I glanced at an open box of face powder, disgusted at how its contents were dumped on the vanity in search of hidden jewels. Next to the vanity stood a tall, Queen Anne-style jewelry cabinet. Empty. Wooden drawers in different sizes lay in a heap on the floor.

"The person who did this took his time," I said slowly, "as if he had an ax to grind."

As if he hated you and wanted you to know it, I thought, keeping my opinion to myself.

"What makes you think this is the work of Matthew Britt?" I asked boldly. "Could there be anyone else associated with you or your husband who might want revenge for something? A business deal gone wrong, perhaps?"

Marjorie stared at me coldly. "I don't doubt there are plenty of people who bear a grudge against Robert. There's a lot of rivalry and back-biting among his business associates and the members of his club. People say one thing to your face, another behind your back." She picked up a crushed, ivory cloche hat with a light pink satin band and blush-colored silk roses, reshaping it with her hands. "But I'm sure this is the work of Matthew."

"How so?"

She pointed to a shelf filled with an assortment of crystal perfume bottles with her initials engraved upon them. Oddly, they'd escaped his wrath. "These are expensive brands, but only one is missing. A brand-new bottle of *Quelques Fleurs*. Still in the box because I received it as a gift and I'm not partial to it. But do you know who is? Betty Britt. She douses herself with it like a whore in church. Matthew was probably so enamored with the prospect of giving her, or one of his lady friends, a stolen gift that couldn't be traced, he ignored the others."

I knew that scent and wasn't particularly drawn to it, but I had noticed it on Betty Britt the evening of her benefit for the Catholic orphanage. The perfume wasn't definitive proof that Matthew had orchestrated the break-in, however, it gave me a place to start.

"All right," I said and turned to leave the ravaged closet. "I'll pay him a visit first thing in the morning."

"No," Marjorie counter emphatically, *"you'll do it now*. By tomorrow, the goods will be gone. He'll have already sold them to a fence, and I'll never get my jewels back!"

But it's the middle of the night, I thought irascibly. I was tired and didn't relish the thought of approaching the Britt home after everyone had gone to bed. One of the neighbors might think that I and my team were up to no good and ring the police. Still…the element of surprise would be an effective way to catch Matthew red-handed if he had the goods. I sighed. "I'll be on my way, then."

Marjorie accompanied me downstairs. Robert was still in the sitting room, pacing the floor.

James stood alone in the foyer, holding my coat and hat, a subtle hint that Robert wanted me out of the house as soon as possible. "Where are Alice and Lou?"

"They went outside, madam," he said stiffly. "Apparently, to snoop around the grounds."

I bid Marjorie goodbye and left to locate the rest of my team. I found them on the west side of the house, discreetly inspecting the flower bed below the trellis with an Eveready flashlight.

"Did you find anything?" I asked.

"Yes," Alice replied walking toward me. "Come and see."

Lou sat crouching on his haunches shining his flashlight on something on the ground nearly hidden between the flower bushes. "Look at this. Our intruder left something interesting behind."

Bending down, I stared at a small white object on the ground. "A cigarette butt?"

"Not just any cigarette," Lou said proudly. "An English brand that only a man of means would buy. Not the choice of your average joe."

I immediately thought of Henry Carpenter, but remembered his style was Turkish tobacco.

"Player's Navy Cut," Lou said with a sniff. "A rich man's cigarette. Costs at least twenty-five cents a pack."

"Holy mackerel!" Alice exclaimed. "I'd give up the habit if I had to pay that much for a smoke."

He held up the remnant of the thin cigarette for me to see in the beam of his flashlight. "This brand is slim and has a distinctive aroma."

"What makes you so sure it was dropped by someone tonight?" I glanced around.

"It's fresh tobacco."

"If it belonged to Matthew Britt, how could you verify that?"

He stood up. "All I need is a quick look at the inside of his fancy rig and I'll tell you if this belongs to him. Traces of it will be everywhere."

"Okay," I said, accepting his hand to rise to my feet. "Let's go."

One cigarette. One careless theft of a bottle of perfume. And suddenly, Matthew Britt wasn't nearly as untouchable as he thought.

Chapter Twenty-Two

Lights shone brightly through the second-floor windows of the imposing brick structure of the Britt mansion as we arrived, indicating someone was still up. Matthew's green Pierce-Arrow Roadster sat parked in the rear, close to the house, a clear sign that he was home.

An older Ford sat at the curb in front of the house, dark and silent, like a ghost in the night.

Lou parked our Model T a short way down the block to avoid being seen if Matthew suddenly passed by a window. We made our way quickly to the back of the house to inspect his car. Alice and I stood guard as Lou opened the driver's side door and leaned inside with his flashlight. After a few moments, he straightened, shut off the flashlight and turned around, holding a small tin.

"We got him," Lou said proudly and held out a shiny, rectangular object in the moonlight. A metal container finished in bright red and cream colors with gold trim along the edges. Across the center, the brand name "Player's Navy Cut" blazed in bold letters beneath a smartly dressed sailor. Lou slipped the tin into his pocket and quietly shut the motorcar door. "There are butts on the floor and the interior reeks of this brand."

We hurried to the front of the house and rang the doorbell several times. Through the glass entry door, the foyer suddenly lit up as someone switched on the crystal chandelier, casting a soft glow over the room.

Ivory approached the door in a dark red robe with a matching turban covering her hair. She yawned and blinked several times, then opened the door, shivering in the cold air. "Miz Char, what in the world are you doin' here this time of night?" she said in a low, worried voice.

"I need to speak to Matthew," I said boldly as I stepped inside the entryway. "I know he's here."

Loud voices coming from one of the upstairs bedrooms echoed throughout the house.

"Look, you promised me, Matt." The female voice shook with anger. "I need that money. Tonight! I barely have enough gas in my motorcar to get to the filling station."

"You'll get it," Matthew said smoothly. "But it's the middle of the night. I need just a little more time, okay, baby? I'll have it for you by tomorrow."

"Don't try to sweet talk me! That may have worked with *her*, but it won't get anywhere with me."

I turned to Ivory. "Who is upstairs with Matthew?"

"I don't know," she stated with a shrug. "My bedroom is downstairs. Mr. Britt went out earlier, but I didn't hear him arrive."

"Ivory, who are you talking to?" Matthew called as he emerged in the open hallway and leaned over the balustrade.

"Miz Charlotte," she replied to him, thankfully only giving my first name. "I'll go and change into something more presentable." Bowing respectfully, she turned and left the room.

To my surprise, Dorothy Bloomer appeared beside Matthew. Her eyes narrowed when she saw me. "What the devil are you doing here?"

I stared curiously, meeting her angry gaze as my thoughts mirrored the same question.

Matthew blinked, as though he didn't trust his own eyes. "Charlotte Johnson—it's three in the morning. Why are you here? I thought you went back to Chicago. Has there been an emergency?"

Leaving Alice and Lou outside, I walked into the grand foyer, a spacious room with a polished stone floor, wood paneled walls, family portraits decorating the walls and a wide staircase with a carved balustrade curving gracefully upward. I stopped next to a round drum table displaying a huge porcelain ginger jar vase filled with blood red silk roses. "We need to talk, Matthew. In private."

Matthew stared at me curiously for a moment, rubbing the reddish, five-o-clock shadow darkening his jaw, then he turned away from Dorothy and quickly descended the stairs. He wore a dark leather jacket and trousers. A folded newsboy cap in dark tweed jutted out of one pocket.

"What's wrong?" He moved close and gazed down at me, his whiskey breath fanning my face. Thick locks of tousled blond curls fell across his forehead as though he'd recently been driving his car with the window open. "You look shaken. Upset. Did you run into trouble with some fella?" His voice had dropped to a deep, almost beguiling tone as he placed his hands on my upper arms, his thumbs massaging lightly. "Don't worry," he murmured, "whatever it is, you're here now. I'll protect you…"

The smile on his face meant to assure me of his sincerity, but something in the way he spoke, in his touch, telegraphed that he had more than *protection* on his mind.

I took a step backward, aware of his true intentions masquerading as chivalry. "You're the one who's in trouble," I said, my voice low and steady. "You're not as clever as you think you are. I know for a fact that tonight, while the Kimballs were out, you climbed up the trellis fire escape and let yourself into their bedroom through the French doors. You stole Marjorie's jewelry."

His blue eyes fixed on me with practiced innocence. His smile turned mocking. "What jewelry? I have no idea what you're talking about."

"You know exactly what I'm talking about, Matthew, so don't feign ignorance with me. You left a calling card at the Kimball house."

Glancing past my shoulder, I nodded to Lou.

He stepped into the house with Alice behind him and produced the cigarette case. "The cigarette butt matched the empty tin in your car."

Matthew burst out laughing. "That doesn't prove anything! Anyone could have dropped it there to frame me. If that's all you've got, you're not very clever, are you?"

"The jig's up, Matthew," I declared, eager to talk some sense into him before the situation escalated. "Robert knows you broke into his house and he's going to retaliate. Don't make things worse for yourself. Give me the jewels. I'll return them for you." I held out my hand. "*Now.*"

He stared at me with distrust clouding his eyes. "What is this really about? Did Kimball send you to seduce me? Catching me in a compromising position would make great blackmail to force me to do what he failed to get when Eleanor was alive—introduction to my late father's social circle. Old money. The real aristocracy in this town." His eyes narrowed. "Tell me the truth, Charlotte. Are you equal partners in his little scheme, or just his present squeeze on the side?"

"I'm not going to dignify that with an answer," I said as the scowl in my voice matched the intensity of disgust in my soul. "I'm also not leaving until I get what I came for. Do yourself a favor and give them to me or I'll have my cousins search every nook and cranny in this house."

He held up his palms, claiming innocence. "Go ahead, search all you want, but you're wasting your time. I don't have them."

"You're lying, Matthew, just like you lied about Eleanor," I said, frustrated. I signaled to Lou and Alice to begin the search. They disappeared into the study. I turned back to Matthew. "You said that in time she'd learn to love you, but she hated you, didn't she? And the night she died, she told you so…"

"She lied to *me*! Both she and her old man. They owe me!"

Betty Britt suddenly appeared at the top of the stairs in her robe. Her salt and pepper hair looked mussed, as though she'd been sleeping. "Matthew," she said to him while staring at me suspiciously, "what's going on here?" She glanced disapprovingly at Dorothy. "What are these women doing in my house at this ungodly hour? Have you no shame? It's disgraceful!"

I glared at him. "Shall I tell her, or do you want to do the honors?"

He shook his head impatiently, waving her off. "It's nothing, Mother. Go back to bed."

"I think not!" she snapped, but then she disappeared the way she came.

I did a double take as Dorothy descended the staircase in a beautiful mauve dress of unmistakable quality and matching fabric shoes that cost far more than a woman of her station could reasonably afford. She looked more like an elite member of the Minneapolis Women's Club than a middle-class woman who earned an average wage. Where did she obtain the funds for such a luxurious outfit? Had she previously borrowed the items from Eleanor, or did she have a lucrative side job to fund her extravagant tastes?

"I see you're still sticking your nose in other people's business," Dorothy said acidly as she walked toward me. "Why don't you go back to wherever you came from and leave us alone?"

"My business with Matthew is none of your affair," I shot back and turned my back on her.

"We can take care of this now, or you can deal with Robert's associates," I said losing patience with Matthew. "He's not going to get his own hands dirty, you understand. He will succeed if I fail."

Suddenly, a heavy fist pounded on the front door so hard it shook the house. With Ivory missing, I went to answer it myself. I had barely turned the latch when Robert Kimball burst in, pushing me aside.

He charged past me and headed straight for Matthew, slamming him against the wall with such force, several portraits rattled loose and fell to the floor.

Dorothy shrieked hysterically and tried to pull him off. Robert shoved her away, sending her stumbling backwards into the stairwell banister.

"You've stolen from me for the last time, Britt," Robert viciously growled, his face purple with rage. "First my daughter's respect, then my reputation at the club, now my property. Give it back or I promise you, I will bury you!"

Matthew's strong hands wrenched his coat from Robert's grasp and shoved him away. "Get off me, old man before I do something I'll regret." He snorted. "Then again, maybe not… I might find it satisfying to wipe that condescending sneer off your face."

Robert staggered back against the drum table pushing the heavy ginger jar perilously close the edge. I darted toward it and caught it just in time, steadying the wide, jar and guiding it back to its proper place. Luckily, the flower arrangement hadn't been ruined.

"You may be younger," Robert warned, "but I know *all* your secrets and a few about your father, too! I could ruin you without lifting a finger."

Matthew's only response was a boisterous laugh to call his bluff.

Ivory suddenly rushed into the room, now in a crisp black uniform covered with a frilly white apron and matching headband. "Goodness, it sounded like an earthquake downstairs!" She scrambled to recover the fallen pictures and place them back on the wall.

The doorbell rang. Everyone turned and stared toward the entrance.

"Lordy, don't you people realize it's the middle of the night? Normal folks are in bed!" Ivory muttered quietly as she left the pictures and went to answer the door. She opened the front door and gasped in surprise. "Miz Marjorie, what are you doing here?"

Marjorie made a sweeping entrance in her full-length mink coat and kid gloves. She looked like her usual glamorous self again with flawless hair and perfectly applied makeup. "I could say the same about you," she said in a breathy voice as she slipped out of her luxurious wrap and draped it over Ivory's arm.

Ivory grasped the coat, running her hand over the thick, soft fur. "After Mr. Robert fired me and refused to give me a reference, this was the only employment I could find."

Marjorie leveled a cool, accusing stare at Robert. "Believe me, it wasn't my doing. I'm glad you found another job, but…" She glanced in Matthew's direction. "Good luck getting paid."

"I beg your pardon," Betty said from the top of the stairs, clad in black velvet, her hair smoothed. Her left arm, still tender from bursitis, hung carefully at her side. "How dare you address my son in such a manner! Your insolence is beyond appalling."

Marjorie looked up, glaring at Betty in disgust. "You? Lecturing me about disrespect? Says the woman who held a fundraiser mere days after my daughter's funeral!"

Betty's face flushed crimson. "Get out of my house, right now—all of you—or I'll call the police."

Suddenly, Robert pulled a revolver from his jacket, eliciting a collective gasp from everyone in the room. "Nobody is going anywhere."

Chapter Twenty-Three

"Now, see here," Matthew said, raising his hands as Robert brandished his gun at us. "Take it easy, old man."

"Ivory, get everyone into the sitting room where I can see them. Now!" Robert barked as he waved his gun around, threatening the people assembled in Betty Britt's foyer.

"You," he hollered at Betty, "come downstairs and get in there with the others."

"This is outrageous!" she sputtered. "Ivory, call the police!"

Robert pointed the gun at Ivory who abruptly stopped and raised her hands. "Not until I say so."

Ivory met Betty at the bottom of the stairs, pushed open the heavy sliding doors and ushered everyone into the sitting room, turning on the lights as she went. I fell in behind Marjorie. The long, rectangular room had cream papered walls, oak parquet flooring and dark, oriental rugs. Tall, mullioned windows were draped in heavy damask, the color of rich wine.

At the doorway, I paused and looked back, wondering if Lou and Alice had heard the commotion. If so, where were they? In another room, phoning the police before Robert could force a confession from Matthew? Or waiting in the shadows for an opportunity to disarm him?

"Get going!"

Robert shoved me forward. I stumbled into the room as he stepped out and slid the heavy doors together behind me, cutting us off from the foyer.

My breath caught in my throat. Why was he isolating us? Had he heard or seen something that tipped him off to Alice and Lou's presence? They had guns to protect themselves, but so did he. What would happen if he confronted them? Without witnesses, it would be his word against theirs.

I shuddered.

Brocade settees and wing chairs in dusty rose circled an oval, mahogany table before a marble hearth. I barely registered it as I sank onto a settee, my pulse racing.

Ivory crossed to the fireplace and turned on the gas to warm the chilly room.

Robert appeared again. He started to close the door, then stopped the moment he saw the fury on Marjorie's face. He went to his wife's side, gripping her chin and jerking her head upward. "I told you not to follow me. How dare you disobey my orders?"

Marjorie slapped his hand away. "To keep you from doing something stupid and making a fool of yourself! I guess I'm too late!" She left him standing next to the fireplace and dropped onto the settee beside me, fuming.

Ivory turned to Betty. "Shall I serve coffee, Mrs. Britt?"

"I'd like some," I announced, raising my hand. "Thank you."

"No," Robert bellowed. "No one is leaving this room until I say so."

Marjorie dismissed the idea with a wave of her manicured hand. "This is no time for teetotaling. I want a drink!"

"Ivory, fix the lady a glass of whiskey," Matthew said, "and make me a stiff one, too."

Marjorie glanced at the bottle of bootlegged liquor in Ivory's hand and grimaced. "That coffin varnish? Absolutely not." She rolled her eyes. "I should have known better…"

"What a ridiculous charade, Kimball," Betty snapped. "Your theatrics are an embarrassment. I hope my neighbors never find out about tonight. If they do, they'll never accept you after this!" She lowered herself slowly in a wingback chair. "What are you accusing my son of that is so reprehensible you need to hold him at gunpoint?"

"You ruined Eleanor's life," Robert said to Matthew with a snarl. He pointed the gun at Matthew's heart. "Admit it or die."

My heart began to thud. I jumped to my feet to intervene.

"Robert, stop this nonsense," Marjorie snapped as she stood and pushed me back down, placing herself in the direct path of his gun. "I have something to say."

She stared at Matthew. "You were in her car, arguing with her when it crashed," she said accusingly. "Don't bother denying it. You treated her like a game of poker. You weren't after her—you just wanted to win the money-prize—her inheritance. And when she rejected you to be with another man, the only option to cover up the scandal was to end her life!"

"That's not true, Marjorie!" Matthew pleaded. "I never laid a hand on her. Especially in her…you know…condition. I'd never hurt her. I'm not a monster! Even though we weren't in love, I cared about her."

"Oh. So…you know about the baby," Dorothy Bloomer said slowly, studying Marjorie's reaction to Matthew's admission.

The disappointment on Dorothy's face caused me to wonder if she'd been blackmailing Matthew to purchase fancy outfits in exchange for keeping Eleanor's affair with Henry out of the society pages. If so, what had she required of Eleanor to guarantee her silence?

But hold on a tick. If Dorothy knew about Eleanor's pregnancy, then she must also have known about the elopement and that Henry would be lost to her for good. Unless, of course, she could get Eleanor out of the way...

I sat in silence, taking it all in as the Kimballs glared at each other, leaving Dorothy's statement hanging. Indeed, the more I watched and listened, the more I learned.

"If this is the hour of truth, then by all means, let's reveal all," Matthew continued in a challenging tone. "You were using Eleanor as payment for passage into high society." He snorted with disgust. "Her death cancelled everything. She wasn't even in her coffin before you cut me off."

"Eleanor's inheritance was the only reason you courted her!" Marjorie snapped. "You couldn't wait to get your hands on her income. The ring was scarcely on her finger when you started chomping at the bit for an advance. You needed it to fund your princely lifestyle because you're broke!"

Betty sat back, scowling at Marjorie. "You're one to talk. We may be short on funds, but no amount of money in this world could cover up the damage *your daughter* almost did to this family's reputation."

I cast a quick, sideways glance at the Kimballs. They looked shaken, upset, but didn't renounce Betty's accusation. They couldn't refute the truth.

"In the end," Betty continued with a sly smile on her plump face, "your good name is all that counts, isn't it?"

Marjorie turned toward Betty with tears cascading down her cheeks. "What does that matter now? Your son has taken everything from me. First Eleanor and my only hope of grandchildren, now my jewels," she sobbed. "I hope you both burn in hell!"

A small movement caught my eye. I glanced quickly toward the narrow opening in the doorway without moving my head, hoping no one else noticed Lou standing in the shadows peering in. I needed to distract Robert to give Lou an advantage.

"Spare me the sermon, Robert, about reputation and high society when you're acting like a low-class criminal by pointing a pea shooter in my face," I said, jumping to my feet. "I've met back-alley bootleggers with better manners than you."

Betty cackled.

"Sit down," Robert snarled, aiming his pistol at me. "And shut your mouth. This is none of your concern."

"I beg your pardon. You're in the presence of *ladies*," Dorothy broke in, clearly insulted. "It's disrespectful."

"A true lady doesn't consort with an engaged man," Robert told her, glancing askew at Matthew. "At least, no respectable woman would."

Marjorie and I protested at once, outraged by the insensitivity of his remark.

"You've got a lot of nerve," Matthew said. "Don't compare her to the cheap chorus girls you entertain every night at the speakeasy!"

Robert shrugged with indifference.

Marjorie stared at her husband with loathing, silent but deadly at his silence. Hurt, anger and humiliation burned in her eyes.

Matthew's gaze flicked from the small opening in the door back to Robert; then he suddenly lunged for Robert's gun. A split second later, Lou jumped into the fray, pushing open the door and grabbing Robert from behind, restraining him while Matthew grabbed the gun. During the tussle, the gun flew out of Robert's hand and skittered across the wood floor, stopping at Marjorie's feet.

She slowly picked it up, stared at it for a moment, then leveled it at her husband's chest.

Alice appeared behind Lou with his necktie, binding Robert's hands behind his back while Lou held him. Robert struggled against his restraints, loudly demanding to be released.

"Come on, Marjorie," Matthew said calmly, stepping toward her and extending his hand. "Give me the gun. You don't want to do this."

"He didn't even bother to deny cheating on me," Marjorie snapped. "Just imagine the gossip this will generate at the Women's Club. I'll never be able to show my face there again. It's high time *I* got the last word."

Matthew grinned with empathy as he reached out and gently pried it from her fingers. "There are better ways to get even with him, you know, and they all start with your lawyer."

In the distance, the wail of several police vehicles pierced the air, the sound growing louder as it came closer to the house.

"Ivory," Lou said quickly. "The coppers are coming. I called them and it sounds like they're not far away. Wait by the door to let them in."

"Yes, sir," Ivory said as she fled from the room.

Signaling to Alice to join me, I rose from the settee. "Nice work," I said confidentially once she stood by my side. "When you didn't appear right away, I knew you two had something up your sleeves."

"As soon as Robert pulled a gun, we made a plan to take him down," Alice said with a proud grin, her gaze flickering toward Lou. "Gee whiz, Miz Char, it was exciting. This job's the berries! I wouldn't trade it for nothin'."

Marjorie suddenly appeared at my side. "Are these people with you?" She asked as she motioned toward Alice and Lou. "Who are they?"

"Lou is my driver," I said, intending to give my team respectability. Only bootleggers and gangsters employed bodyguards, and I certainly didn't want to give anyone that impression. "And Alice is my secretary. She's a whiz at typing and shorthand." I smiled at Marjorie. "You should get one. She's invaluable."

"Really," Marjorie replied, studying Alice with interest. "She could use a good tailor. Does she do calligraphy?"

Suddenly the sirens interrupted our conversation, becoming

deafening as the police cars stopped in front of the house. I followed the stampede into the foyer. Outside, the echo of boots crunching on the snowy sidewalk in front of the house sounded like a small army.

Dorothy hurried to the hall closet and grabbed her long, wool coat. "Matthew, I must leave. If this incident gets into the papers and I'm named as one of the individuals present, I could lose my job at the library. We're warned to keep our noses clean or face removal." She held out her hand. "I need gas money."

Matthew reluctantly reached into his pocket and pulled out two dollars.

"Thanks. I'll keep in touch." She snatched the money from his hand and hurried down the hallway to the back door, slipping into her wrap along the way.

Ivory opened the door and admitted two uniformed officers. They filed into the house, each man stamping the snow off his boots as he entered. The room became noisy and crowded. I stood on the wide stairway to get a bird's eye view of the proceedings. Alice and Ivory joined me. Betty stood in the sitting room doorway, ignoring us.

"Mr. Britt," one officer spoke, "what's going on here?"

Robert began to bluster, demanding he be released instantly or his lawyer would swiftly retaliate. Matthew and Lou attempted to explain, over Robert's protestations, what happened and turned over the gun to the officers.

One of the officers bumped into the drum table but quickly steadied it. "Excuse me," he said, making me regret not pulling it aside when I had the chance. The once beautiful arrangement of roses in the ginger jar now looked messy and disorganized.

"Miz Char," Alice whispered. "Come with me to the library. I found something I'd like to show you."

Slowly, we made our way along the edge of the crowd until we reached the short hallway that led to the library, a room paneled floor to ceiling in dark mahogany with oxblood velvet draperies, Persian carpets, and a marble fireplace. Leather-bound volumes lined the walls with a rolling brass ladder resting against the shelves. Off to one side stood a claw-footed partners' desk. The faint scent of old cigar smoke lingered.

Alice pointed to a music box resting on an oak side table. The tiny porcelain bird, painted with soft, natural colors, perched on top. When wound, it let out a sweet, tinkling melody that filled the room like a whisper of spring. "I don't know why," she said, puzzled, "but I keep seeing this bird everywhere I go. At the hotel in St. Cloud, there was a picture of a nightingale on the wall. Under it, a little plaque said the nightingale symbolizes independence and courage."

She held up the little box with a smile. "This is you!"

I smiled back. "The Nightingale Detective Agency!" We began to laugh. "Is this what you wanted to talk to me about?"

"No," Alice replied as she put the music box back. She went to a small table in one corner and picked up a large Bible in black leather, cracked with age. It fell open to the division between the old and new testaments to reveal several pages with a handwritten record of family lineage. She pointed to the entries, now faded with age, the sepia ink penned in an elegant, looping style.

One glance told me everything I needed to know.

"What are you doing in here?" Betty's sharp voice cut through the air. We spun around to find her standing in the doorway. "How dare you riffle through my personal things? Get out before I call to the police and have you arrested for trespassing!"

Alice and I quickly left the library and headed for the foyer again. As we stepped out, I looked back and saw Betty snatch a small wooden card box off the desk. Looking for her attorney's telephone number, most likely. The Kimballs would probably be willing to pay a very tidy sum to keep tonight's activities out of the society pages.

"This is an outrage! I demand you release me at once or there will be consequences!" Robert's voice boomed across the foyer, naming influential people he could call to intercede in his arrest and demanding that the police search the Britt house for *his* stolen merchandise.

Marjorie stood off to the side, silent, glowering, smoldering with anger—no doubt over Robert's humiliating penchant for chorus girls.

Matthew stood next to Lou by the stairway with his arms folded, inviting the officers to search his home, claiming they wouldn't find the items in question. Either he'd stored them offsite or he really was telling the truth.

One officer restrained Robert as the other one began to search. I went to Lou and stood next to him. Looking around, I accounted for everyone except Ivory and assumed she'd gone down to the kitchen to make coffee for the police. And, hopefully, the rest of us. A steaming cup of joe sounded mighty good right now.

"They won't find anything," Lou whispered to me. "Alice and I combed this floor already. There's a wall safe in the study, but it's open—and empty."

I moved up a few stairs, watching the room from a higher advantage. Why was Robert so adamant that his property was here? As the thought lingered, my gaze fell on the disheveled silk roses. They looked bunched up, as though someone had jerked them out and shoved them back into the vase. I ran down to the drum table and seized the flowers in both hands, yanking them out. At the bottom of the vase lay a heavy cloth bag.

My gasp drew Marjorie's attention. Her eyes widened as she reached into the vase and pulled out the thick cloth bag, filled with something heavy. She peered into it and let out a sigh of relief. "It's my jewelry!"

"See!" Robert shouted. "I told you he robbed us! Officer, arrest this criminal and untie me, now!"

"He's lying!" Matthew responded, shocked. "I've never seen that bag in my life."

Marjorie stared at the parcel, looking confused. "Why are they in your banker's bag, Robert?"

"I don't know," Robert grumbled. "He probably grabbed the first thing he could find to make away with them."

She frowned. "But these bags are only kept in your desk, and it's locked all the time." She looked up, fuming then stomped toward him, slapping his face with a thrust that made him reel backward. "You stupid fool! Pulling a stunt like this just to get even with the Britts. You knew how much my mother's heirlooms meant to me, but you didn't care about my feelings, did you?"

"You got them back unharmed, so why are you upset? I had to find some way to get even with him for destroying Eleanor's life," Robert said angrily.

Marjorie winced and took a deep breath, as though struggling to deal with all the stress and humiliation he'd caused her. "You destroyed my beautiful closet," she said with tears in her eyes. "Or did you assign that piece of dirty work to James, your faithful stooge? Well, you can sleep with him from now on, or one of your filthy chorus girls because I'm moving into Eleanor's bedroom as soon as I get home." She shook her fist in his face. "I hope the coppers throw the book at you!"

The scene between Marjorie and Robert made me uneasy. We shouldn't have witnessed their marital breakdown. It was personal and none of my business, but I couldn't help thinking that Robert got what he deserved. To spare her further discomfort, Alice and I busied ourselves rearranging the flowers, carefully slipping each stem into the frog, a thick glass disk pierced with tiny holes, at the bottom of the vase.

Marjorie went into the sitting room with the officer in charge and dumped the contents of the banker's bag onto the table to make sure everything was accounted for. She called on Ivory, as a former employee, to sign a written statement, swearing that the jewels were hers. When Marjorie finished with the officer, she surprised everyone by giving Betty her ring back.

Back in the foyer, Robert still maintained his innocence, insisting he had used the jewels only to give the police cause to search the house, believing they would uncover the diamond bracelet which would prove that Matthew had been guilty of a worse crime—abandoning Eleanor as she lay dying. Had the name of the person in question been anyone other than Britt, Robert might have managed to sway the police. But Robert had underestimated the reach of Betty's late husband, a former ambassador. Her word, her standing; his miscalculation.

Betty went into the library to call her lawyer, screaming as she went that she planned to file charges against him.

"I'm tired, Charlotte," Marjorie said, a faint crease forming between her brows. "I'm going home to pack my jewels away and retire. My maid, Ruby, is restoring my closet. She should be finished by now."

I didn't bother asking her why she wasn't accompanying Robert to the police station or calling their lawyer to represent him; I already knew the answer.

Marjorie turned to Lou, smiling through her exhaustion. "Would you be a dear and start my motorcar? It's devilishly hard to crank in this cold."

"What a great idea," I said, letting Lou know I didn't mind if he started her car first.

"I'll warm up the Tin Lizzy," Alice added as she followed Lou out of the house.

"What do you think happened to the missing perfume," I asked Marjorie as my team left. "It wasn't with the jewels."

"Oh, that," she replied with a wave of her hand. "Ruby found it under a pile of skirts. It had fallen off the shelf."

Well, that cleared up another issue. But there was one left. Who was in the car with Eleanor when it crashed? Who robbed her and abandoned her as she lay dying? Knowing what I knew now, the answer was clear. And it was time to get justice for Eleanor.

Chapter Twenty-Four

"Marjorie, there is something I think you should know," I said in a low voice as we stood off to one side in the Britt's foyer watching her handcuffed husband, Robert, protest his arrest as he argued with Matthew and the officers. "Even though Matthew is innocent of the theft, I believe the pawn ticket for Eleanor's bracelet is in this house."

She stared at me, her eyes widening with shock. "Are you sure?"

I nodded. "Alice came across something in library that convinced me. We need to find that ticket while everyone is distracted. And when we do, we'll have proof." I described to her what we found.

She suddenly perked up, as if my words gave her a burst of energy. "Well, then, let's go. Let's search every nook and cranny."

"I need to ask Ivory something first," I said in haste.

I found Ivory hanging the fallen pictures back on the wall, fussing over the damage to the beautiful foyer. Next to her, a large, cracked indentation in the plaster indicated where Robert had slammed Matthew's body into the wall. Small chunks of plaster and fine dust covered the marble floor.

"I'm so sorry about the mess," I whispered to her. "If I were Betty, I'd demand that Robert reimburse me for the repairs." I picked up a beautiful landscape painting and handed it to her. "Ivory, I need your help. Where does Betty store things that are personal or valuable?"

Ivory gave me a curious look. "In her bedroom, ma'am."

"Thank you!" I leaned close. "Don't mention this to anybody."

I returned to Marjorie, motioning her to come with me. "Lou and Alice searched the entire downstairs," I said as we bounded up the servants' staircase at the back of the house headed for the master bedroom. "If the ticket had been hidden anywhere on the first floor, they'd have found it."

Except for rumpled blankets on the elaborate four poster bed, the room looked spotless, making it easy to search. Marjorie dumped out Betty's handbag, but the ticket wasn't among the items in the bag. We searched the walk-in closet, fanned the pages of the books on her night table, looked under doilies, Tiffany lamps and even the oriental rugs, but our search produced nothing.

"Look at this," I said as I reached into a mother-of-pearl jewelry case hidden in the back of a dresser drawer and unfolded a small, pre-printed form. "I found it."

Marjorie snatched it from my hand. "Great Scott…"

"Well, that explains how she bankrolled her lavish benefit," I said under my breath, remembering the rich canapés, desserts and never-ending supply of giggle water that night. "I wonder what else she pawned." Looking around, I noted a blue Murano glass vase and handblown crystal figurines on her dresser, trying to remember if I saw anything like it at the pawn shop. "This place is full of costly treasures."

"Hello?" Betty called from the bottom of the grand staircase in the foyer. "Ivory, is that you? I told you to make me an egg and toast. What are you doing upstairs?"

We left the bedroom and stealthily made our way back down the servants' stairway again. Entering the foyer, we approached Betty from behind. She spun around, looking baffled then confused to see us come from that direction.

"What are you still doing here? Everyone has gone. I thought you were following your husband to the police station," Betty said, pointing to the window. Outside, our automobiles idled at the curb, surrounded by a cloud of exhaust.

Marjorie gave a sharp, humorless laugh. "His attorney can coddle him. I'm done playing the fool."

Betty glared at us with impatience. "Why are you still here? What do you want? I'm in a hurry."

"I imagine it's difficult slipping into clothing with that sore arm," I said, ignoring her question and touching my fingertips lightly against her left shoulder. "Perhaps it's worse than you've let on."

She winced, backing away. "Don't touch me!"

"I've heard that bursitis is uncomfortable, but I've never seen anyone with a shoulder as sore as yours," I said calmly, a sudden clarity settling over me. The truth had been there all along, but I'd failed to discern it. "It isn't bursitis at all, is it? The truth is, you dislocated it when you were thrown from the car."

"I don't know what you're talking about," Betty snapped and moved toward the stairs. "Now, get out. Both of you! My lawyer's coming over after breakfast. I need to get ready."

"I've pieced together what happened," I said as she turned away, dismissing us and starting up the stairs. "The night Eleanor died, she came here to tell Matthew the engagement was off. You heard them arguing and called Robert, didn't you? You couldn't let the goose with the golden egg get away. When he showed up the three of you turned on her, and that's when Eleanor admitted she was going to marry Henry because she was in love with *him* and was having his child."

Marjorie gasped at the sound of my words. Her face turned ashen, her eyes filled with fresh tears, but she didn't ask me to stop. So, I continued.

"You knew she was going straight to Henry that night to elope," I said, raising my voice. "But you couldn't allow that, could you, Betty? When Eleanor left the house, you followed her to her car. You were the one that the old man, Whit Crosby, heard arguing with her just before the car went off the road."

Betty stopped and turned on the stairs, staring down at us with a sneer. "You have no proof of this. You're just guessing!"

Marjorie held up the pawn ticket, snapping it open. "This is the receipt you signed with a false name at the pawn shop for Eleanor's bracelet."

"Perhaps Eleanor gave it to me," Betty said smugly, "in exchange for a favor."

I shook my head. "You didn't know her very well if you think that lie would fool us. And even if she did, why use a false name? Because you stole it and needed to protect your secret. The jig's up, Betty. Mamie Alsobrook is listed in your Bible as your mother!"

"I didn't steal it. I found it on the floor of the car." Betty's cold eyes studied us with a deliberate, calculated stare. "Let's go into the library," she said descending the stairs, "and discuss this like adults."

I wondered why she didn't take Eleanor's engagement ring as well but then realized that Eleanor's fingers were probably too swollen from her pregnancy to get the ring off.

Betty reached the bottom of the stairs. "The crash was an accident, but it served my purposes. Eleanor's elopement would have made a laughingstock of me and my son. I couldn't allow that cheap little doxie to ruin my good name by making her indiscretion juicy fodder for drawing-room gossip. I'd never be able to show my face at the Women's Club again!"

She shepherded us into the library and went straight to the fireplace, turning on the gas. "It's chilly in here." She walked to the door. "I'm out of matches. I'll be right back."

Marjorie and I exchanged curious glances, but before we had a chance to respond, Betty shut the door behind her. A key turned in the lock with a deep *click*.

Footfalls tapped on the marble floor as Betty hurried away.

We ran to the door and tried to force it open, pulling on the doorknob, but it refused to turn.

Marjorie leaned against the door, her eyes blazing. "I saw that key in the door when we came into the room, but it never dawned on me that she'd use it to lock us in. That stupid fool! Wait until I get my hands on her..."

I turned toward the fireplace. What was that soft hissing noise? The air permeated my nostrils with a sour, rotten egg smell. "Marjorie, the gas is still on."

We raced toward the fireplace and got a rude surprise. "Where's the key?" I glanced around, looking frantically for the skinny brass piece that fit into a small escutcheon plate on the floor to regulate the gas flow.

"She must have taken it with her," Marjorie said, looking around for something to use. "Maybe I can use a letter opener or a pair of scissors to turn it. Something strong…"

We searched the room, but nothing useful turned up that fit the size or shape of the hole in the plate. Meanwhile, the acrid odor intensified.

The front door suddenly banged shut.

"Betty just left the house!" I leaned against the door, closing my eyes as lightheadedness overtook me. Approaching the window, I ripped open the curtains. I tried to open it, but the window wouldn't budge. So, I jumped up and down, waving my arms. Hopefully, Lou or Alice saw me signaling them.

"I'm feeling sick," Marjorie said placing her hands on her chest as she began to cough. "I need to sit down."

"Ivory!" I pounded on the door with all my might. "Ivory! Help! Are you there?" I made enough noise to wake the dead, but it didn't bring Ivory to our rescue.

I'm not going to die this way, I thought stubbornly. *I need to raise my children, to be a good example for my sister and my staff. And my darling, Will… We're supposed to grow old together! What am I going to do?*

A tear formed in the corner of my eye. Kicking the door so hard I bruised my toes, I continued in desperation to scream for Ivory.

To my surprise, the front door opened again, followed by heavy footsteps.

"Lou," I cried out, pounding on the door, my head swimming with dizziness. "Is that you? We're locked in the study!"

"Miz Char," Lou's deep voice rang out as he rattled the handle. "Yes, it's me!"

I fell forward against the door in relief, banging my forehead. "Oh, praise God!"

"Move away. I'll kick it open."

"Wait," I cried as a fit of coughing overtook me. "The gas is on with no fire, and we can't turn it off."

"Just a minute," he said and walked away. A sudden blast of cold air seeped under the door, creeping along the floor like a dense, icy wave. After a few moments he returned, inserted a key in the lock and slowly, carefully, unlocked the door. As it gently opened, frigid air rushed into the room making me shiver.

He grabbed me by the shoulders. "Are you all right? The smell in here is enough to make me gag."

I nodded with relief. "I'm all right. I just need some fresh air."

"I found a key in the door to the lower level," he said with a nod. "Ivory was locked in, too. She's getting your coats."

"Thank God." I sucked in a deep breath. "Where's Betty?"

"Gone," Lou said, taking my arm. "She asked me to help her board Mrs. Kimball's car to wait for her. She said you were getting your coats on. As soon as I closed the door, she scooted across the seat and drove away! I came into the house to find out what was taking you so long and if she had permission to take it."

I filled him in on the latest developments as he assisted me into the foyer and handed me off to Ivory.

"Ivory, get your coats," Lou said. "I've got to go back for Mrs. Kimball."

A few moments later he returned with his arm around Marjorie's waist, easing her down on the stairs. "You ladies need to leave at once. I'll fetch a valve key from another room and shut off the gas before it blows this place to smithereens."

I slipped into my coat as Ivory helped Marjorie with hers. Then the three of us, arm in arm, slowly made our way out of the house to an overcast sky and the tawny light of dawn. Thick, white flakes fell in earnest, making the sidewalk slippery as a skating rink. Alice met us as we descended the front steps and helped us navigate the rest of the way. Ivory, Marjorie and I climbed into the backseat of my Ford and pulled a thick wool blanket across our laps breathing a collective sigh of relief.

Lou slid into the front seat next to Alice and slammed the door. "Where to," he asked me, leaning back and resting his arm along the top of the seat. "Your house or Mrs. Kimball's?"

"I want my car back," Marjorie snapped in a sharp, bitter voice. "I know how Betty thinks, and she's heading straight to her lawyer's house! As if *he* could save her from all she's done. Go after that thief!"

Alice stepped on the gas, navigating the car along Mount Curve Avenue, following the wide tracks that Marjorie's car made in the new snow. "It's kinda slippery," Alice said. Both hands firmly gripped the steering wheel. "But I'll catch up to her. She's never driven a truck through a muddy field pullin' a full hayrack or hauled steers to market in the pouring rain. This is easy!"

The snow came down faster, making it difficult to see the road. Lou kept a portion of the windshield clear with a small hand lever that operated the wiper. After a few minutes of treacherous driving, the road angled sharply to the right. We kept moving, convinced that Betty had gone that way as well.

"There she is," Lou remarked, pointing to a single red taillight glowing faintly ahead of them. "She's weaving all over the road."

I leaned forward, craning my neck to get a better look. "That car is behaving exactly like the one that nearly hit us the night of the benefit."

Alice and I exchanged quick, knowing looks.

So, today is the second time Betty has tried to kill me, I thought angrily.

We kept a respectable distance, but the stolen motorcar sped up, swerving worse than before.

"She's crazy, driving that fast," Alice remarked and reduced speed to keep my car from sliding. "If she doesn't slow down, she'll cause an accident!"

Up ahead, a policeman stood in the intersection of Mount Curve Avenue and Douglas Avenue wearing a dark coat and hat, white gloves and a metal whistle on a chain around his neck. Tall elm and oak trees arched along the road, standing bare against the gray sky like sentinels in front of silent, stately homes. The odor of coal smoke from their chimneys filled the air.

Blowing his whistle, the officer held up his hand for traffic in our lane to stop. Alice applied the brakes and the car began to fishtail on the icy road. Ahead, Marjorie's car swerved wildly, too.

"Hold on!" Lou cried gripping the dashboard.

Our car slowed then stopped, but Marjorie's car kept going.

"She's not going to yield," Lou said as we watched her car swerve straight into the officer's path. He jumped backward to avoid being hit, falling onto the street.

A chorus of horrified exclamations filled our car as Betty sped past him.

A car going west on the cross street entered the intersection, but it didn't stop. It didn't have time. I watched in horror as it plowed straight into Marjorie's car, smashing the driver's side.

And the driver.

Chapter Twenty-Five

November 23rd

Large, fluffy snowflakes drifted lazily from a leaden sky as Ethel and I made our way past massive granite monuments, stone angels, and skeletal trees in Lakewood Cemetery to our motorcars after Betty Britt's interment. The rolling hills, winding roads, and snow-covered gardens felt more like a vast, hushed park filled with historical markers than a cemetery.

The service for Betty was held in the extraordinary Byzantine-style Memorial Chapel. Its red granite walls, curved roof tiles, and bronze doors gave it the appearance of a small European cathedral. During the service, I sat in awe of the breathtaking interior, finding it difficult to concentrate on the sermon. My gaze kept drifting upward to the soaring mosaic dome glimmering with gold, marble, and colored glass assembled from more than ten million tiny pieces crafted by Italian artisans who had worked at the Vatican.

Betty's sendoff was every bit as lavish as her life.

Alice and Lou followed us at a discreet distance, dressed to blend in seamlessly with the crowd. Lou wore a dark suit beneath a leather jacket while Alice looked striking in a long wool coat over a new black dress and fur-lined boots.

"That was a wonderful tribute to Betty, wasn't it?" Ethel asked me as she pulled the printed memorial from the pocket of her fur coat. "I must say, though, I was surprised to see that she was only fifty-three."

She stared at the pocket-sized paper with raised brows. "She looked a lot older."

"I imagine she had her share of problems," I replied and shoved my gloved hands into my coat pockets. "Worrying, especially about money, can age you quickly if you let it get to you."

"If the gossip I've heard is true, her son no longer has financial concerns," Ethel replied. "At least, not presently." She shot me a sideways glance. "Word around the Women's Club is that years ago, Betty's late husband saw to it that they were both well insured. Their home is expensive to maintain, and he probably purchased the double policy to ensure that when the time came, Matthew could afford to keep it." She gave an emphatic harrumph. "I suspect he knew Betty would make short work of his portion and be left with very little by the time her own policy came due. Their son will be fine as long as he steers clear of the gambling tables…"

"Speaking of Matthew," I said to change the subject, batting snowflakes from my face, "Ivory is staying on with him for a few weeks before she comes to work for me. He's selling the house, and he's asked her to hire a team of household staff to get the place ready for a huge estate sale."

Ethel chortled. "It'll be the event of the year! We should make a day of it. You, me, and Marjorie. We'll hit the sale in the morning, have lunch at the club, and then end up at my house for late afternoon cocktails."

"All right," I said, smiling. "Let's do it! Now that Marjorie and Robert are living separate lives, she's loving her independence. Did you know that I've arranged for her and Henry Carpenter to meet next week?"

Ethel did a double take. "Is that so?"

"Henry made reservations for dinner at the Granite Club Supper Room in St. Cloud. Marjorie really wants to meet him. She has many questions about his relationship with Eleanor."

Ethel's eyes began to mist. She cleared her throat. "I'll miss that young lady."

"I believe her death was the final straw for Marjorie," I added. "When she realized how much information Robert had deliberately withheld from her, it was the ultimate betrayal. It changed her. Then finding out about his penchant for chorus girls drove the last nail in the coffin of that marriage." I shrugged. "She'll never be under his thumb ever again."

"Surprisingly, Marjorie and Robert managed to remain civil long enough to agree with Matthew to bury the truth of Eleanor's and Betty's deaths with them to preserve their memories," Ethel remarked.

"Both Ivory and I swore to it, also," I said solemnly. "Marjorie offered Ivory her old job back in return, but Ivory declined." I shook my head. "I can't say I blame her."

"I didn't see Dorothy Bloomer today," Ethel remarked. "It must be true what people are saying about her and Matthew."

"According to Ivory," I said, shoving my gloved hands into my pockets, "she miscalculated whatever hold she believed she had over him. Now that he's been exonerated of Eleanor's death, he's cut her off entirely and told her never to show her face around him again."

"Don't look now," Ethel murmured, "but I believe we have a budding romance in our mist."

"Really?" I was dying to look behind me to observe Alice and Lou firsthand but didn't want to embarrass the lovebirds. "What's going on?"

Ethel grinned. "They're holding hands…"

I smiled, thinking of how far Alice had come since the day I found her in the alley behind my office. She was sweet, sharp, and capable of far more than she'd ever given herself credit for. All she had ever needed was someone to believe in her. In the end, that someone was me—and Lou.

Ethel and I reached the roadway, pausing to say goodbye before parting ways.

"Why don't you join me at the Women's club for afternoon cocktails?" Ethel asked with an encouraging smile. "We'll warm up with hot cocoa and a shot of good brandy from my flask."

"Gosh, I'd love to, Ethel, but I have to pick up Francie from school," I said regretfully. "Will is taking us out for dinner tonight to celebrate solving my first case, and she needs time to get her studies completed before we go. Otherwise, they won't get done."

"Ah, the joy of young people," Ethel replied with a sigh. "I remember those years well with my own sons. Clarence needed little prompting, but the younger one, Alvin, was a challenge." She patted my hand. "Some other time, then."

I said goodbye and joined Errol in the limousine with Lou and Alice, turning my thoughts to Francie and the evening ahead.

*   *   *

"You're late," I complained to Francie, checking my watch as she climbed into my husband's favorite motorcar, a bright yellow Packard Roadster. "School got out fifteen minutes ago!"

She hated having Errol pick her up from school in the limousine because its presence prompted jokes from her friends about riding in a bootlegger's "liquor wagon." I didn't mind taking the Packard. I loved driving and rarely got the chance nowadays.

"I was talking to my friends and lost track of time," Francie said as she slammed the door and dropped her canvas school bag on the floorboard. She wore a sky-blue wool coat and a matching felt cloche hat. She pulled out a pocket-sized mirror and checked her appearance. "Golly, I need to take a bath and fix my hair before we go to dinner. I'm going to wear a new dress!"

"First you need to complete your studies for today," I said to my sister, trying not to sound like a nagging mother. "We have reservations for seven, so you have plenty of time to study *and* get dressed."

Francie let out a labored sigh. "Don't be such a fuddy-duddy, Char. I'll get it done—" She suddenly shrieked. "Look out!"

I swerved just in time to avoid hitting a dog darting across the road. The lanky, light brown canine missed my front tire by mere inches. "Oh, my gosh," I said, breathless. "I almost hit it!"

"Pull over, Char," Francie cried with a trembling voice. "I need to make sure it's okay."

I veered to the side of the road, sweat prickling the back of my neck, my hands shaking so hard I could barely manage to steer the car. Francie jumped out and sprinted across the road, returning with the dog clutched in her arms. I feared the worst.

"It's just a pup," she said as she opened the car door and placed the dog on the seat. Climbing in, she pulled the trembling animal onto her lap. "He was shaking like this when I approached him, but he doesn't seem to be hurt. It's obvious he's a stray." She pointed to the dog's ribs protruding and the bony ridges of its spine as a tear fell from her eye. "Look how skinny he is! Poor baby. I need to bring him home and feed him. Cook will help me fatten him up."

"I know your heart is in the right place, but Francie, you don't have time for a dog. We've already been through this—"

"Then I'll make time," Francie argued as she possessively hugged the pup. "He needs me! I'm going to call him Pal. He can stay with me at night. During the day, he can be with Captain."

Captain, a huge German shepherd, belonged to our gardener, Rory. The dog followed Rory around all day and prowled the grounds, guarding my property at night. Would he accept a companion?

The pup's large, sorrowful eyes stared up at me and melted my heart. I couldn't leave him behind.

*   *   *

Later that day…

Will entered the bedroom dressed in a smart navy suit and bold cologne as I applied the finishing touches to my makeup. Standing behind me, he placed his hands on my shoulders. "Ready to go?"

"Yes. I'm looking forward to it," I said and stood, sliding my arms around his neck. "This is the first time we've gone out to dinner in weeks."

Will circled his arms around my waist, pulling me close. "Francie's waiting downstairs, but I wanted a minute alone with you first." Bending me backwards over his arm, he engulfed me with a deep, passionate kiss. "I'm so proud of you, my darling. You did a terrific job of solving your first case."

Yes, I did, didn't I? I thought to myself and couldn't resist smiling as my thoughts turned toward the future. Now that I had 'The Nightingale Detective Agency' added to my name on the door of my office, perhaps I should place an ad in the St. Paul Pioneer Press to tell the world.

The Nightingale Detective Agency was open for business!

The End

But wait…

If you liked this story and want to read more about Char, I invite you to continue her journey in **The Bootlegger's Wife**, book one of the Moonshine Madness Trilogy. To get started, you can read the first chapter here:

https://www.deniseannette.blogspot.com

If you just want to go straight to the book, you can find it on Amazon.

About the Author

Denise Devine is a USA Today bestselling author who has had a passion for books since the second grade when she discovered Little House on the Prairie by Laura Ingalls Wilder. She wrote her first book, a mystery, at age thirteen and has been writing ever since. She loves all animals, especially dogs, cats, and horses, and they often find their way into her books.

She has written twenty-two books, including books in the Beach Brides series, Moonshine Madness series, and West Loon Bay series. Her books have hit the Top 100 Bestseller list on Amazon and she has been listed on Amazon's Top 100 Authors.

If you'd like to know more about her, visit her website at:

www.deniseannettedevine.com

More Books by Denise Devine

Christmas Stories
Merry Christmas, Darling
A Christmas to Remember
A Merry Little Christmas
A Very Merry Christmas - Hawaiian Holiday Series

~*~

Sweet Romance
The Encore Bride
Lisa – Beach Brides Series
Ava – Perfect Match Series
Della – Enchanted Island Series

~*~

Moonshine Madness Series - Historical Suspense/Romance
The Bootlegger's Wife – Book 1
Guarding the Bootlegger's Widow – Book 2
The Bootlegger's Legacy – Book 3

~*~

The Charlotte Van Elsberg Cozy Mystery Series
The Nightingale Detective Agency - Book 1

~*~

West Loon Bay Series – Small Town Romance
Small Town Girl – Book 1
Brown-Eyed Girl – Book 2
Country Girl – Book 3 - ***Coming soon!***

~*~

Christmas in West Loon Bay Series– Small Town Romance
Once Upon a Christmas – Book 1
Mistletoe and Wine – Book 2

~*~

Cozy Mystery

Unfinished Business
Dark Fortune
~ Girl Friday Cozy Series ~
Shot in the Dark – Book 1
The Accidental Detective – ***Coming Soon!***

~*~

Forever Yours Series - Inspirational romance
Always is not Forever – Book 1
This Time Forever – Book 2

Want more? Read the first chapter of my novels or get my complete book list at:

https://deniseannette.blogspot.com

~*~

Audiobooks Galore!

Do you like audiobooks? Many in the list above are available in audio!
Check out Denise's website for links to each audiobook.

https://www.deniseannettedevine.com/audiobooks

Narrated by Lorana L. Hoopes
Monthly sales!